About the author

The author is trying to defend Nature against mankind. The extinction of animals, plants, fungi, are so far underway, he must, he says, name and shame the culprits, as his enemies. Forests and oceans are under siege. The author has lived and worked in many countries, and found people everywhere to be good hearted, adaptable, creative, and yet narcissistic in the sense that they put mankind first, and consume the planet for reasons they can invariably justify. The great religions of the Earth, and science itself are no exceptions. The author writes in hope of change.

HUMAN ZOO

Stubbsy

HUMAN ZOO

Vanguard Press

VANGUARD PAPERBACK

© Copyright 2024
Stubbsy

The right of Stubbsy to be identified as author of
this work has been asserted by him in accordance with the
Copyright, Designs and Patents Act 1988.

All Rights Reserved

No reproduction, copy or transmission of this publication
may be made without written permission.
No paragraph of this publication may be reproduced,
copied or transmitted save with the written permission of the
publisher, or in accordance with the provisions
of the Copyright Act 1956 (as amended).

Any person who commits any unauthorised act in relation to this
publication may be liable to criminal prosecution and civil claims for
damages.

A CIP catalogue record for this title is available from the British
Library.

ISBN 978-1-83794-005-9

This is a work of fiction. Names, characters, businesses, places, events
and incidents are either the products of the author's imagination or
used in a fictitious manner. Any resemblance to actual persons, living
or dead, or actual events is purely coincidental.

Vanguard Press is an imprint of
Pegasus Elliot Mackenzie Publishers Ltd.
www.pegasuspublishers.com

First Published in 2024

Vanguard Press
Sheraton House Castle Park
Cambridge England

Printed & Bound in Great Britain

Dedication

Herbert Jones

Acknowledgements

Animal Farm

CHAPTER ONE

Bingo owns a Zoo. Large, and swart, he squints, and squirts perspiration, eyes agleam like Benzene, chin shiny, face sallow, save for a place high on the cheek, a spot of unnatural cherry pink. "Let me tell you a story," he says, and sips wine through purple lips.

His story is about a magic pot, which on instruction cooks ready meals. This little parable sits plumb in the middle of my mind, abstaining from digestion. Another metaphor. What is it with Bingo and his circus?

I was getting nowhere trying to raise funds in the City. The financial markets were lame. The market in rare species was going through the roof. Red wolf pups, prime number cicadas, death-stalker scorpions, bamboo rats, Malabar civets, flat-back turtles, mindoro crocodiles. A Camudi snake is worth thirty pairs of shoes in Bond Street.

As part of my programme, I go round the big companies shaking my tin. Chairmen offer introductions, but not much cash. Bingo referred me to my best donor, Venetsianov. He is, Bingo said, an Oligarch. Turns out he is a Silovarch, who sidestepped sanctions.

He does not grant audiences. So I am fobbed off with his fixer, Grigoriev, prematurely old, thin lipped, prurient, who had, it seems, a wish to be a Taipan. He suffers from Nostalgie de la Boue, a brownish delicacy of his youth. With mawkish sentiment, he catches the eyes of strangers across crowded rooms, hoping they will prove susceptible to his leadership. One object of his affection is a bully called Gowler, a boorish character. Together, Grigoriev and Gowler run Venetsianov's Empire. Brute force occupies their minds. Desperate to see his wishes enacted before he pops his clogs, Grigoriev chose Gowler as his enforcer. He admires him.

Venetsianov made land-grabs in the Ukraine, but hid his tracks. In Russia, he picked up land at low prices, foreseeing fortunes to be made in agriculture. But only five percent of Russian land is arable, they say. In the end, his henchmen grated on the Putinistas. Neither of them have any idea of strategy or understand finance. Throwing your weight around is no substitute for knowing how things actually work.

My life was about to change. I was writing a book entitled *Percy Shelley's Pangolin*; subtitle: *A Python, a Puma, a Bat, a Bee, and a Bird.* The book was PR, but no publisher is willing to cut one down for my purposes.

"I had to lay out £20,000 for newborns today," said Bingo. "I do swapsies."

"Meaning?"

"I swap old rhinos for more sexy items."

"My business is high tech. On my computer, facial and olfactory recognition; locations; extinctions; futures;

short positions. You could do worse than market my gizmo. I will make it worth your while."

"You could be driving up the price of replacements. Thought of that?"

"In terms of deaths, mosquitoes come tops, and there's Covid and other terrors of the biome. But for sheer quality of death, my top ten are: hippopotamus, saltwater crocodile, polar bear, blue-ringed octopus, anaconda, poison dart frog, box jellyfish. The price of crocodile is soft. Sharks' fins firm."

"You have a Polar Bear?"

"'I can pick up Polar Bears from the Russian Islands by the dozen,' so Venetsianov tells me. I don't want them. They're trouble. I've had two. One killed the other; then a keeper."

"Dear, dear. What else you got?"

"African buffalo, Komodo dragon, black mamba, fat-tailed scorpion." He breathed on lustrous fingernails.

The etymology of Zoo suggests life. But Bingo is into the Thanatopsis of a sleepless Zoo.

When I first got to England, I was invited to a talk at the Royal Society. The subject was Darwin.

Vast aeons, small, innumerable changes were his coinage.

After the lecture, I introduced myself. "Thank you," I said. "I'm no scientist. Out of the grand total, how many species have survived to date?"

"Mankind is the driver of extinctions," he replied. He laughed archly, then explained, "We are conditioned to accept extinction. Darwin wanted us to think, as Copernicus and Galileo did before him, but on the matter of extinction he clearly failed.

"Darwin had the effect of making us less concerned with metaphysics, and more anthropocentric. If he had debated with Aristotle, nature would have been better served."

"Yet he was a great man?"

"I have a soft spot for Hoyle," was his reply. "He saw earth as a tiny outpost peppered by meteors, carrying viruses, and bacteria, which, taking up residence on our planet, were refreshed thereafter by a continuous stream of genetic information. But let me be clear: this does nothing to lessen Darwin's undying fame."

"So, no reservations?" I asked.

"Nothing." He winked…

What a curious fellow, I thought. Playing devil's advocate like that.

"Evolution," he said, "is actually the product of Nature in its entirety, not some dull process obediently followed by molecules.

"The Environment evolves, not life. Like Fortune, the Environment changes endlessly. It grows, it writhes, it morphs, it vanishes. Life, as we define it, clings on, desperate to survive. From this angle extinction is misfortune, not the sorcerer's apprentice. Life, desperate life, an opportunist, uses every tool to hand to save itself in a frenzy of slow motion.

"We are too ready to tolerate this epidemic of extinctions.

"But this is just a personal foible," he said. "The Royal Society will drum me out if you report me."

Surprised, I thanked him, and left.

These ideas, like moths, took residence in my mind, and made holes in my conception of life. "Are we riding on a wave of extinctions?" I asked the taxi driver. He did not reply. We traversed strange streets, unrecognisable and dark. The meter mounted up. Uncertainty crowded my mind. We were taking the long way round, but uncomplaining?

Back in my digs, I quietened down. The machine of life progresses. No need to fret. God, who, they say, guards time itself, is unperturbed, and largely absent. Darwin's thesis perhaps needs spring cleaning. The jewelled component of a metaphysics unintelligible and unfamiliar, a mere pause between moving parts. Darwin conceived a colossal system, which would transform man into the great moral creature he alone could become or maybe is. And yet…

A few weeks later, Venetsianov threw a party at a club near the Natural History Museum, to mend Anglo-Russian relations.

As the bash was warming up, I whiled away the time talking to Hugo, my Annie's dad. Anything to do with fish or fishing is up his street. And nowadays he has a part-time role tracking the Russians and the Severoput passage.

"How's your project?" he asked. "Trees, isn't it?"

I played this like an Englishman, with a straight bat.

"The problem is biodiversity: what has been lost?"

"These are scientific matters," he replied.

"The sea may be our last chance," I said. "The UN predicts a third of farmland will disappear worldwide. Could we enclose the oceans?"

"Of course not. The same old criminals top the overfishing list: China, America, Russia, Japan, India. Knock out too many species and you cock up nutrient recycling. Annie knows more about all that than I do. Personally, I would farm seals," he said.

"Fat, aren't they?"

"Soak them in salt water and strip out the blubber. Ask the Esquimeaux. The common seal cannot be beaten for juiciness and digestibility, and is very, very warming. But the blue riband goes to the leopard seal. Their brains are the real deal, sliced thinly and served on hot buttered toast. Liver and heart also delicious."

Oh, dear. Is it any wonder biodiversity is tanking?

Just then, Bingo breezed up and offered a pudgy hand to Hugo. "Let me introduce myself. I am the Zoo Meister, Adlergesicht, protecting the wild as it fragments." He showed his front teeth, as of a donkey braying.

Then Venetsianov drifted alongside like a plutocratic yacht. He hailed us in his lugubrious voice. "There is something sad," said he, "when you people can't guess your impact on the planet."

"Our friend here is asking about fish farming, your worship," said Hugo.

Venetsianov frowned and moved on.

Bingo winked. "The world is emptying," he said carelessly. "My goal is to fill my boots. Of course, I get the stuff about global warming. But see how one medium-sized war does for the best-laid plans."

***

A week later, Venetsianov summoned me. As I eventually discovered, he likes to be thought a Prince.

"I am here to take notes," I said. "But once I have heard your wishes, I hope you will find it in yourself to help."

"No-one has spare cash at the minute," he replied. "Seek out Lord Toot of Tooting Broadway. Mention my name. Known him for ever. Make sure you see him before noon." He winked.

"The other man I like is the Chairman of Mooti Foods," he added. "They have no strategy. So refreshing. Yet the City support him mindlessly. Why? He lends his name to any and every Ponzi scheme. As a result, his galleon is followed by a vast fleet of imitators. Get him on board and your coffers will fill up. Now then. No time for gossip. To business. You are an expert of the rain forest," he said.

"No, no. My experience is Brazil, Venezuela, Guyana, the Andes. I know deforestation is critical if we are to lower emissions; 3.6 gigatonnes of carbon dioxide, to be precise."

"Of no importance. I have an estate; the size of Wales. I finance Mr Bingo in exchange for an occasional favour. I defer to his knowledge of the frozen North. He is splendid, a sort of Frankenstein who tragically traverses the wastes of dying Nature."

"In Russia?"

"I refer to Gowler. He knows the territory, from Arkhangelsk to the Pole."

"Where Angels fear to tread? An arctic Darwin?" I said.

He sniffed. Then admonished.

"Darwin, who claimed that evolution is progress to perfection? Such idealism."

Tell that to the Dinosaurs, I thought.

Venetsianov has a small round face – and was small in other ways, with a bright skin and soft little lips. His wife is heavy featured, ugly, but he treats her like the personification of romance. I take off my hat to him. I imagine he gives her rare animals to mark their anniversaries.

"Forests are the earth," he said. "You know, seventy-five percent of all known species inhabit rainforests. Though they account for less than ten percent of the earth's surface."

"Where do the oceans fit in?" I asked.

"Every rain forest is an ocean. Have you heard of the Ussuri Tiger? The giant Manchurian Tiger? They build shrines to him. Twenty-two foot long."

"I have not, I am afraid."

"My estate is so immense, it dwarfs the Amazon. In it we have forestalls. We forest. My land was designated Zapovednik, by Putin himself.

"These are Boreal forests, named after the God of the North wind. Greek, did you know? We Russians inherited our religion from Byzantium. Christ is our legacy, my legacy, while you British neglect the spiritual life."

Who does he think he is?

"The Ussuri Taiga are Rain Forest," continued Venetsianov. "I am talking of the Primorski Krai and Khabarovski Krai. I am talking about the largest forest on earth. I am talking about the Sikhole-Alin Mountains. Seen by the brave. In it fly the huge fish owls, and in it run the grey wolves.

"My place is in birch woods not very distant from Primorye. You can get there by train." He smiled in a calculating fashion. 'You are now my pawn,' he seemed to say.

"And of these Godlike Tigers there are five hundred left. Chinese medicine has decimated them. The Chinese are muscling in. My scientists say diversity in the Primorski Krai is pathetic; only twenty-five Tigers have balanced genomes."

"I thought the Chinese were your friends," I said. I knew he played a role mediating between the Chinese, the Russians, and anyone else seeking alliances against America.

"You know the tigers' genome?" I asked.

"I intend to capture the viable ones. A tremendous task. Like climbing Everest in the 1950s. Their future is in my hands. I identify with them."

"Yes," I said.

I looked at this small fellow, and felt compassion for the Amur tiger.

"As a world leader, Stalin was head and shoulders above the West," he added. "It is difficult to get a true picture of him, in the recent blizzard of disinformation."

"Do you regret Ukraine?"

"A few things. You live in a tiny island. Russia is immense. It embraces a vast range of places, peoples, climates, time zones. It withstood the vilest invasions from Europe. Look at casualties in the great wars. Who won? Was it Belgium or Russia? You tell me."

I was unimpressed.

"The future depends on an atavistic struggle between huge forces. In this confrontation, Russia will determine who comes out on top. Speak to Grigoriev."

"I have. Tell me, what brings him here?"

"A temporary arrangement. How did you find him?"

"I got little from him."

This was not the answer he required.

"An old-style bourgeois, a cold man, a nitpicker. But efficient. Did you meet his Growler Orlik?"

"I did."

"A tough, eh? I need tough people. Nato is still desperate to invade our homeland. America scammed us of wealth and tries to starve us. We oppose the Western idea of migrants, who kill and rape yet are protected, we don't know why. We stand for the rights of Russians to resist fanatics in Chechnya, and the East. Men like Gowler are invaluable."

"Is logging a problem for you?"

"Don't talk to me about morality. I am totally moral. While your bourgeoisie have – what do you call it? – scrubbed up, that is to say over-washed yourselves until your pink skin is devoid of immunity – all by the simple colonial device of destroying forests everywhere, in order to plant palm trees and make acres of excess soap. It is the hordes of the effeminate West that export pain and famine to the world. Palm oil and washing are the enemy of biodiversity. You clean by killing wildlife.

"You cannot clean your souls. The great Ussuri river on the Chinese border flows through the monsoon, and through the freezing fog into the Amur river, which shares its name with Leopard, and with Tiger, and fills the Sea of Okhotsk.

"My gift to Russia is my Tigers. I make a reserve for them, and, in parallel, I breed a super-race under controlled conditions, by bringing in twelve breeding pairs for improvement."

"Not gene editing, I hope?"

He ignored me.

"You will go there and see these majestic creatures, not only majestic but divine, and advise me how I may achieve this goal. And while you're there, consider the lovely ambient temperature that awaits Russia on the morrow. We will be tropical.

"Money is no object. Take this credit card. Do what you have to."

This was a good opportunity to study the Russian forest. I bought a ticket on the Trans-Siberian Railway and met Gowler for a briefing.

"Once there, find Eleniya," growled Gowler. "Her father is on our payroll. Pass her this personal letter which is sealed with my mark. Understood?"

I headed for Berlin.

East of Berlin, in a perfectly good train, I was reading up on mental health. Psychiatrists adore the suffix 'phobia' and use it to describe anxiety disorders. In America, phobias are a common mental illness amongst women; and in Sweden, women are twice as likely to suffer phobias as men (26.5 percent versus 12.4 percent) Women are four times as likely as men to have a fear of animals. That goes back to hunter-gatherers, I guess.

Great care must be taken to leave analysis to professionals. Otherwise, things are misconstrued by media and politicians alike, who turn everything to the purpose of abuse. Xenophobia as opposed to Cenophobia has been corrupted to mean hatred (not fear) of foreigners. Gordon Brown would know, poor fellow. I am an immigrant myself. A brief survey of history shows Britain was first to become dependent on foreign food. This led to deprivation, not least for young men, sent out to the extremities of the world to live on the margin of survival.

How the real world works requires empathy, rather than political insults, so often directed at loyal, moral citizens. There are still people who attach high importance to the family, and its preservation. Venetsianov questions promiscuity at the expense of family. He says this is exacerbated by social media promoting sexual preferences, which are of no concern to him, but could be analysed objectively.

A similar schism exists in nostophobia: the rewriting of history for political purposes. This is based on the idea that history is mere opinion. Used to decry the past, it scorns nostalgia, the meaning of which ranges from celebrating the homecoming of heroes, who faced death for their compatriots, to yearning after joyous memories. Finally, I came across Phobophobia, which means being afraid of being fobbed off. Believe me.

CHAPTER TWO

In Primorski Krai, in fact in the City of Primorye, I met with Venetsianov's people. I looked for this Eleniya, but she was not there. We planned to trek after the Tigers. Before long, I began to wonder at the enormity of the task. I got on well with local scientists and wildlife experts. Eventually, I was assigned a young guide, who turned out to be Eleniya Arseniye, fresh-faced, petite, inclined to laughter, who treated me with great respect. Against my better judgement, I fell in love with her.

I tried to reason with her. "You must be religious, living in Nature as you do beside the glorious river, Kiyevka."

"So-called by the Ukrainians," she said.

"Water," I replied, "is precious, life-giving, mysterious. Springs, streams, rivers were worshipped as gods. The pools in which we swim are now impure. Each wind was worshipped. Mother Earth itself, worshipped. Animals were possessed by gods," I said.

"Yet man ate them?"

"Animals were totems."

"We are wiser now," she replied.

"Water, air, life itself are in our genes."

She was an inspirational guide to the area. She showed me the enormous pines and massive hoary spruces which, pressing on all sides, overhung the wilderness and the paths which unreliably threaded the vast forest.

It was three months before I realised the capture of preferred animals over vast distances was impossible.

What was inescapable was that the Amur Tiger reigned over the land. He is quintessentially Russian, capable of withstanding solitude. Icy cold and gnawing hunger were his comrades. The idea of capturing him was mad.

We settled for darting any tiger we could approach, holding it in a temporary cage, analysing its genome remotely, in the hope it would conform to target; before transporting it into further captivity.

The Natural world re-entered me. Like an elixir, it made me immortal, transporting me to my youth.

I had occasion to visit Eleniya's parents in a poor homestead on the margin of the forest. Her father was a forester, her mother looked Korean. I tried to communicate my intentions. They showed hostility. There were, they said, religious obstacles.

I was getting nowhere. So, although I did not wish to marry her – this seemed impractical – I decided to ask her anyway, as the best, if not only, way I might show my feelings.

She said no. I pressed her. Again and again she resisted.

On one expedition, I was injured. We found a tigress, set a trap and darted her. I had no reason to suppose this would not tranquillise the animal completely. It seemed to work. The tigress, losing consciousness, swung a torpid paw and though it missed anything important, a claw caught my trouser and ripped the flesh on my calf.

There was pandemonium. I was hospitalised. Eleniya was upset.

I remember a stranger, ramrod straight, who ordered others to take care of me. I cannot recall his face. But I filed the memory under the name of Sentinel.

When I was discharged from hospital, Eleniya came to me and told me my feelings were reciprocated. But, she said, there was something I had to take into account. She took me to a hide, not that far from her parents' place, and told me I must spend the night there, and keep watch. It was to be a sort of trial. Beyond this, she refused explanation. On no account could I fall asleep or try to exit the hide. I made such undertakings, but still she insisted on manacling me in such a way that I had no possibility of escape. She then furnished me with an alarm clock, set it at three in the morning, and instructed me to take a pill at that point to ensure I stayed awake for at least two hours thereafter.

I did not understand any of this, but wanted to show willing, unconditionally, to please her. On the evening in question, she took me to the hide and I embraced her. I still remember the scent of her. She smelled of larch, birch, pine, and spruce all mixed together. And I, who am a creature of woodland, was in heaven. "Watch everything tonight," she said.

At the appointed hour, the alarm went off. I roused myself and looked out through an aperture at the forest. It was a moonlit night, but in addition a small torch suspended from the hide cast a low light on the clearing outside. An hour later, there was movement. And at that moment an enormous tiger walked slowly towards me. This was surely Hu Lin, the King, the giant Manchurian Tiger. He came up to the hide. He sniffed deeply. I froze. Then he lowered his head, out of sight.

A long pause ensued. There was no sound. I did not move. Then the Tiger turned and walked away.

There was a scratching at the door.

I opened it. There was Eleniya.

"That was lucky," I exclaimed. "I have travelled hundreds of miles and failed to find him. He was here all along."

"I know," she said.

"You knew? All along?"

"Yes," she said. "He came to see me."

"To see you? I don't understand."

"He just came up and smelled me."

I went cold with fear.

"He rejects me."

"How?"

"My grandparents are people of the forest. I was promised to the Tiger."

"They would feed you to him?"

"No. I was promised to him. If a Tiger has an eye on a girl to make love to her, she must decide yes or no."

"Decide on what? How do you know?"

"We judge from our dreams."

"We? Who is we?"

"My parents, my grandparents. They say since certain vows were made for me, it is now impossible for me to marry a man. The Tiger came and smelled me and rejected me."

"Why did he not kill you? Why did you submit? Anyway, you don't need to do as they tell you. Do what you want."

"I am sorry," she said. "It is too late. I have given myself to him. In my dreams I long to make love to him, the spirit in the shape of Tiger."

I understood immediately. She, an uninhibited girl, longs to make love. But ill served by parents whose job it is to help her, she is vulnerable.

My mind turned to other things. I became hypersensitised to the forest. We went on trekking. We camped out amongst the rocks and always built a huge fire to keep animals away at night; then failed to find them by day. Eleniya no longer came with us.

She did come at last. "I have brought you a gift," she said, and handed me a foul-smelling heap of rags. In it something moaned.

"What is it?" I asked.

"A baby."

The camp fire flickered on the rocks. I peered closely. I just made out the sight of a starving animal.

"What is it really?"

"A wolf cub. The Tiger killed its mother."

"A curious gift, Eleniya. How sad that you should see this as a baby. Do one thing. Have it cared for. I will find it when my job is done."

She left. I thought no more of it. I listened to the local guides, who talked of Tigers as if they are gods. The Tiger, they said, helps and protects the gorals, the Sika deer, the martens, the hares. The bears are his subjects. He took me to a bear cave. There was evidence of occupation.

"Sometimes, a Tiger comes here."

"You mean...?"

"He is the predator of bears and wolves. He eats Black bear, Brown bear, he eats Grey wolf."

And then a bolt came out of the blue. Eleniya died.

Why? How?

I felt such misery. There is a rumour, they said, that the Tiger comes and lays upon her grave.

I had difficulty sleeping. Half awake, half dreaming, I wondered if my destiny was to submit to the Tiger; yet I hunted him. I was like Ahab.

At the same time, I turned past events over and over in my mind. I could not control my memories of Eleniya, how we longed for each other's company, how I neglected her.

Eventually, I sought out a Shaman to break the impasse. I saw her fallen in a trance. I heard the sound of grey wolves and birds of prey and I was told they were helping nearby.

The Shaman awoke and told me of a winged tiger which, she said, contained a great spirit. And she called out to tiger cubs which were visible to her but invisible to others.

"I am the tiger Shaman," she said. "A tiger may be your brother or brother-in-law. If in your dreams a tiger shows attention to you, you will die."

"Is this what happened to Eleniya?" I asked, but she did not reply.

So I decided at last, in a kind of apathy, to trek that Tiger. The lead scientist tried to explain that there is no evidence this is his territory. But my guide reported otherwise. "There are two or three bears around here," he said. "One lives in that cave. There has been a new tiger sighting. Very big, and hungry."

Interestingly, we ended up at the hide where Eleniya had taken me. The team had a goral tethered to a post. Dart guns and an eight-gauge gun were held in reserve. We settled down to wait.

Two days passed. I was ready to go back to Europe. Then, to my surprise, I was roughly shaken out of sleep.

"Our bait has been stolen," they said, and I was told to look. A huge bear was dragging the goral away. Just at this moment, with bewildering speed the Tiger appeared as from nowhere and leaped on them. His ferocity and torque threw the bear down and he was at his throat, tearing at the windpipe. And then I saw the Tiger commence his feast. This is a mystery beyond understanding.

One thing survived this melodrama: my love for Eleniya. To call it unrequited is self-pity. I was unmanned. Why had I not pressed my love more ardently? I was fascinated by her because she was, in my mind, the wild. I associated that forest with events which epitomise the paradisiac dream of nature.

The cub she gifted me had died.

To my astonishment, the team found a replacement. Its bones were forcing their way through the skin. It stank, but I smuggled it home. I had no option, but would give it to Bingo's Zoo. There it would be fostered by a sow, who, they claimed, had suckled a lion years before. Fostering is in nature, says Bingo.

After Russia, I felt disconnected. A whole stretch of time remains incomplete, like a dream in which the dreamer is missing or is a silent but impotent observer. Tigers link our lives. She entered his life; he hers.

Later, Venetsianov would make the comparison. The Tiger, he will say, is paramount. He is all-powerful in Nature. His is the sovereignty of flesh. While mankind fails in his duty to the natural world, the Tiger governs. Animals accept his power from which flows death, which is ever-present. It cannot be hidden. He controls predation, so maintains stability. He is King, and governs accordingly. Without him is anarchy and unnatural death. You, like a pestilence, interfered in my forest, then vanished.

This Venetsianov would say.

CHAPTER THREE

I made my peace with Gowler, who was upset at Eleniya's passing. I put up with a tirade as if it was all my fault. Half Dutch, half Russian, he has problems deciding which. This time he spoke for Holland.

"Our leadership in technology is second to none," he said, "in agriculture, in water management.

"When sea levels rise, our skills in land reclamation will be in demand across the world. Schliemann was shipwrecked on the way down from Hamburg, but able to stand for a few hours on a sandbank in the middle of the North Sea, till he was rescued by a passing boat, and resumed his road to Troy. For us, this kind of merman existence is second nature. Sandbanks are Holland. Climate change will raise sea levels. Then, perhaps, a species pump will conserve us as a sovereign species.

Our beliefs are cultivated over millennia. You think that racist? I think it a sign that we are special.

"Come now," I said (the man seemed self-obsessed).

"No, no; think about it," he insisted. "Darwin has much to teach us. He tells us how we may evolve.

"Look at it another way: if you save one child from sexual exploitation, that speaks to what is natural and good in humanity, does it not? Don't let bureaucracy suppress outrage when children are defiled. Bureaucracy hides debasement.

"New traits are characteristic of emerging species. We Dutch created our identity by invention, by reclaiming Polders better than any nation. More important is the civilisation we created."

"Be careful not to demonise others," I said, "or to unleash nationalism."

He looked angry at this (anger or pretended anger was his forte). "Bureaucrats," he said, "prefer immigration. It dilutes genomes. As Darwin astutely said, innovation is evolution. He did not beat about the bush. Species that fail, he said, go under. This is the tenet of evolution. Consider margarine."

"Margarine?" I said, surprised.

"The industry was pioneered in Holland. Margarine is superior to butter. At this very moment, the dairy industry is an obstacle to carbon reduction. Emissions from butter are three and a half times those of margarine. Just as we step up in the battle against global warming, the margarine industry is sold under our nose; although, as Dutchmen, we are best equipped to face the challenge. Palm oil plantations in Indonesia have shrunk the rainforest by an acreage equal to that of New Zealand in its entirety. But in Holland we have technologies to source oils elsewhere."

"Such as?"

"Mealworm oil, or even algae. We can use genetic engineering to produce edible oil from tobacco plants and from fish farms. Anyway, global warming will change climates, thus opening up huge swathes of territory to new plantations. Margarine is a marvellous vehicle for nutrition.

"But to do all this, top class intellects are needed. The recruitment of the best management from other industries is necessary, and investment in science must be raised to new levels."

Gowler now looked distraught.

"Why am I saying this? Because I am a Dutchman. My margarine industry has been sold off. Yet I was the right person to meet that challenge.

"The analogy is with natural selection. If humans do not cope with global warming, humanity itself will go extinct.

"In our country, we have a national discourse on precious assets. If floods come, we manage them better than others. If agriculture enters a crisis, we are equipped to deal with that, too. But watch out for bureaucrats. They have no strategic insight. They fail to value the skills required. They favour recruiting more of the same. They do not understand science.

"Ants evolved as farmers, biologists, builders, soldiers, each programmed to work on his specific task. The parasol ant imports fungus into its nest to practice agriculture. This happened millions of years ago. Nowadays, it is not uncommon to see a file of ants in the Dutch Antilles marching up the kitchen wall, across the ceiling and out the window, each carrying a cornflake.

"Their *raison d'être* is to feed the queen and her offspring, and so expand her empire. They fight for her.

"Fighting is essential. Humans also face perpetual struggle. Leaders fail. In desperation, they hire consultancies and these fail. Chief executives fail. Governments rely on civil servants who, risk-averse, add little or no value. The answer is the alpha male."

"Like you?"

"Like me. Failure edges us towards extinction. They bureaucratise operations to trim costs, then are horrified at what they have done. Like ants, we Dutch are farmers, builders, also scientists."

Gowler, distracted by his opinions, was crude, direct, but not quite right.

CHAPTER FOUR

I personally do not understand evolution, and I have no insight into the extinction of animals underway.

I decided to remedy this. A good starting point is Bingo's Zoo. I asked if I could set up camp there. At least temporarily.

Ulysses, the head keeper, agreed. I start next Monday.

I was lying next morning upon the grass, examining the English sky. High, high above, a little object rose into the aching void, then arced and fell. Down, down it came, a distant speck against the white enceladine. It was a lark singing in headlong flight. Fluttering, mystic runes imprint my senses. Larks are in decline. They whirl in circles down from slow vertiginous haunts, uncurling like music, unfolding, sliding, descending, for the moment free, unmindful of the owls and shrikes and men who crave their evanescent flesh.

Since Edward I, merlins were trained to hunt the skylark. Why? What gave birth to such profanities? A tiny creature caught throughout history by men, often dragging nets across the grass and trapping the nesting birds at night. Since Roman times, men have sought to pluck out little tongues for greedy pleasure. Even the tiny skylark is abused. What is it about birds' tongues? They are a sort of finger, capable of dexterity, articulation and the acoustics of lovely songs. But edible? Only man could think so.

Man cannot fly nor sing so well. Like an asteroid, he threatens life. What if an asteroid in the shape of a billion humans were to fall upon the world below? Isn't it? Won't it? Larks' tongues are as good as kingfisher nestlings to the imported mink. They have no rights, their primal purpose and design perverted. Are we not to live by aetiology? If not, is every human child a work in progress in the fabrication of new monsters? Now I am motivated to protect larks, trees, plants and forests.

Ulysses, the manager of the Zoo, agrees to enable my research.

"What do you want to study?" he asks.

"Primates? A group big enough to reveal the benefits of captivity?"

"I've just the thing: baboons. They have a big enclosure. Everything is peaceful. There are nine of them, and they seem to relate well."

I made notes and after three hours went to the cafeteria for tea.

Ulysses appears.

"Learn anything?" he asks.

"I got the impression of a settled group. Presumably, the top baboons have a job for life."

"No. I can unseat anyone. In the wild, things are less predictable. The hierarchy is down to testosterone, stress and politics.

"The top baboon has elevated testosterone and depressed glucocorticoids (stress hormones), depending on how stable his group is. He gets first dibs on food, sex..."

"What is his life expectancy?"

"Can't say."

"What does his tribe think?"

"Most are submissive. You could say they like to be bossed about and like to see the top man boss the others. It's like working in a multinational from what I hear. A minority want to be boss. He has to keep the rest onside. He does them favours; sucks up to females and babies. But it pays him to create instability, as this makes him indispensable."

In between studying baboons, I took an interest in a penguin. She swam about in a huge pool, the sides of which were transparent so you could see what she was up to under water. Her name, I was told, is Adele, and she has the reputation of bossing her mate and chattering at him. Ulysses claims she is promiscuous, but his only evidence was that she collects rocks to make a hypothetical nest and if she sees any male penguin with a rock about him she offers him sex in order to get her beak on his rock. This struck me as somewhat removed from human behaviour. But then she is cooped up in a zoo.

Adele was very attractive and uninhibited. One day, I found her lying in a pool of blood with part of her missing, presumably eaten. This shocking discovery brought home the importance of zoo security. An animal had broken in and killed her, maybe a stoat or a fox.

She and her mate were going steady, and their attachment was quite touching. Suddenly, the real world appeared; the zoo is a human fantasy which shortens life by human error and carelessness. Poor Adele. Yet Adele and her mate prove love in penguins.

I tried to do a post mortem. It turns out Adele was on medication.

"What for?" I asked Ulysses.

"Zoochosis."

"Meaning?"

"Depression. Stereotypies. She was on antidepressants and antipsychotics."

"Where did you get her?"

"Hamburg, if my memory serves."

I thought she might be suffering.

"What was getting her down?"

"Could have been a thousand things."

CHAPTER FIVE

I have a Ghanaian friend, Yamhead by name. Occasionally, he brings a delicacy for me to sample.

Walking through the Zoo, I was savouring his latest offering, when I caught sight of what I took to be a Jaguar. Back home, I would have called her a Tigress, but after Russia, Tigress was too grand a word. This Jaguar was small with magnificent markings, not infrequently favoured by city blondes.

I called out "Hello!"

To my gratification, she gave every appearance of hearing me. She seemed to say: 'Read the sign, can't you?'

I spoke in my native tongue. "Sorry. Haven't seen you before."

With a twitch of her tail, she paced the enclosure, golden eyes periodically meeting mine.

"I can't see a sign," I said. "I am guessing you're from the North, aren't you?"

On low-slung haunches, she turned her rear on me.

"You look as if you might hunt rhea on the Argentinian plain. I would say you're from a forest."

She turned round. "You're getting warmer," was her reply.

She was giving nothing away until she knew me better.

"Are you in danger of extinction?"

"Not in here I'm not. Shall I join you? We can stroll around this Zoo together?"

"If that's OK?"

A few visitors looked embarrassed, presumably at the sight of someone talking loudly to himself. Some of them grinned, others looked sympathetic at the indecipherable animal noises.

Their derision brought our conversation to a temporary halt.

Shortly afterwards, I was approached by a beautiful woman. I looked at her inquisitively.

"Yes," she said. "Here I am."

"So you are. I am delighted to find we're on the same wavelength."

"You seem very much at ease within yourself," she remarked; "and if I may say so, you're rather handsome."

"Help me out here," I said. "I have been under some stress recently, and am only too aware the mind plays funny tricks."

"Then where is the animal that was here a minute ago?" she asked, pointing at her empty enclosure.

"Must have gone inside," I said.

"I am short of words," she said; "it's lack of practice. How about a burger?"

"Of course. Let me show you…"

"Sometimes I go for days without eating, although in this place the food is good. I'm not fussy. I can get by on insects, even worms. But it's not like home."

"And where is home?"

"Guyana."

"No! Me too!"

"I don't believe it. Give me a curassow and some cassava bread any day."

"Or a turkey? Or a labba?"

"Then we could fall asleep under the awarra? It's nice to meet someone from home. To tell the truth, I have no idea why I'm here. It's all a bit of a game, isn't it?"

"They're trying to make the place more exciting. You fit in well. You look cool."

She giggled.

We wandered off to the canteen and ordered burgers, a Coke for me, some water for my companion; and we sat down to talk.

"My story," she said, "is uninteresting."

"Hardly. You're the national animal of Guyana, and the emblem of the Argentinian rugby team. Yet there is something of the forest about you."

"That's perceptive. I don't like zoos. I'm not mad keen on the idea of being locked up. Since the dawn of time they have enslaved us. Some even married us. In Tabasco, I'm told, there are ancient carvings of faces half human and half Jaguar."

"It's a long time since I spoke with a Jaguar. Are you familiar with the word Shaman? Are you one?"

"Come now," she said. "Do you remember the story of the Jaguar and the crab?"

"The crab took its eyes out and threw them in the sea?"

"Go, eyes of crab, go, go. Into the middle of the sea, go, go," she cried.

"And then the crab used magic to call them back. The crab warned the Jaguar. 'Never take your eyes out,' he said. 'Never throw them in the sea, or sharks eat them.'

"But he did. He took them out. 'Go, eyes,' he called, 'go to the middle of the sea. Go, go.'

"And the shark ate them. So the Jaguar became pitifully blind."

"Until, thankfully, a piamen took the yellow gum from the briars and helped him make replacements. And that is how, Jaguar, you got such beautiful golden eyes," I said.

She blushed. "How nice to make a new friend," she said.

"Tell me, when you turn yourself into a human, are you still jaguar? Put it another way. Have you ever fallen in love with another jaguar?"

"That's personal," she replied.

Strangely, I no longer saw a jaguar but a star. I felt instarred, and sensed Eternity.

"This Zoo is colonialism," she said. "Images of hunting everywhere. Images of hunting dogs, bows, arrows, fire, nets, snakes, poison."

"Actually, we are quite safe here."

"Don't you believe it," she replied. "What brings a charming man like you to a provincial Zoo?" she asked.

"I am not entirely human. Back home, I would be called a tree spirit. I am here on an assignment."

"Oh? COP26?"

"How come you know about that?"

"It's surprising what you pick up from visitors. If you're interested in ecology, are you expert in evolution?"

"I can't make head or tail of it."

"Then waste no time. Extinctions are gathering speed. Interview some of the animals here, and you will get it. Only then should you turn your attention to the forests. I can help you there. Now excuse me, I must get back inside. My name is Satin." Then she left.

I might just have fallen in love. A chance meeting. I might as well fall for an animal, passing off as human. Here was an opportunity to learn.

This is the most significant thing to have happened to me since I got back. I have made contact with an animal and fallen for an alien, created long before modern man evolved. Suddenly, I found myself talking to animals, even insects, and in some cases getting replies.

I did, for a moment, wonder if my indulgence in Yamhead's substances was affecting my mind. But love is love. You know it when you've got it.

I reported to Venetsianov.

"I am grateful to you," I said.

"Why?"

"I learned a lot."

"And…?"

"Your project could take twenty years."

"Why so long?"

"The Tiger is elusive. If you were to ban logging, it would help."

"That would cost too much."

"It would be worth every penny."

"Get America to fund it. Do I detect in you an attachment to wild things? In Russia, people come first.

"Let me explain," he said. "We have entered a new age: the age of coercion. Balance of power is a thing of the past. We Russians are impervious to the old alliances. Instead, we craft new ones with those who cannot trust the West. China, India, Turkey, Brazil, Iran. The West is terrified of us. We make propositions you can't refuse.

"Our boreal forests up in the North are the biggest land-based carbon store on Earth. They store more carbon than there is in the atmosphere – and twice as much as humans created over a hundred years. More boreal tree cover has been lost to fire recently than anywhere else on Earth.

"Now, Russian trees are marching North. They march across the tundra and, with warmth on their backs, they thaw the permafrost and release carbon in catastrophic quantities.

"Our temperatures are running away. We invite you to save the world, our world, by solving this. We, Russia, have other concerns of planetary importance. We are tending to the Severoput.

"So you must dance to our tune, and dance attendance upon Nature," he said. "You must deploy the assets you have stolen from us. Your sanctions bled Russia dry, yet you demand we invest in greening for your benefit.

"We command you to make a sacrifice. If you obey, you may have access to the Boreal, the arctic and Severoput. If you refuse, on your heads be it. Welcome to the age of coercion."

"Have you resolved your problem with Ukraine?" I asked.

"Russia can never be denied access to the Black Sea," he replied. "This logic eventually will sink in. Toynbee explained it all in 1916."

"But you are the aggressor?"

"Russia is the victim," he persisted. "The West is the 'arch-aggressor of modern times'. Invasions of mother Russia in 1610 by Poland and Sweden; 1709 by Sweden; 1812 by Napoleon; 1853 by Britain, amongst others; 1915 by Germany; 1918 by Western powers trying to overturn the revolution; 1941 by Germany.

"In these invasions, the blood shed by Russians is oceanic. Poles and Ukrainians acted as agents of the West. Our civilisation confronts them. We banned publications in the Ukrainian language, you banned Gaelic. We protected the most holy church and its patriarchy by moving it out of the Ukraine. Just as you tried to supersede the Roman church. We controlled the wheat harvests in Ukraine for the benefit of humanity, just as you controlled the Highlands and islands, and Ireland itself, when it suited you. These are footnotes. Do you know Solzhenitsyn, much loved by the West? Given the Nobel prize, was he not?

"He was a megalo.

"He, like Toynbee, showed Russia always included Belarus and the Ukraine. Imagine Wales, the Highlands and islands. Imagine them stolen from you in 1991 by an opportunist Atlantic power. You can't, can you? My forest, which interests you, is Russian, not Ukrainian. Russians won the last War. Europeans cannot be trusted. Our people survived starvation, massacre. We lead the world in art and science, you know?"

"Yes," I said.

"The Russian is not like your effeminate leaders, who bribe people with minimum wages, with sexual exceptionalism, who indulge them with human rights they do not even understand. No, we protect ourselves against the West, which, if it has its way, will simply kill us. Watch the West teeter when COP26 collapses." He wiped his mouth and continued, "The papacy conspired to destroy the Orthodox church. But who believes? Not the West. We learned long ago the sinews of Christianity are Empires. I, too, have a need to be charitable."

CHAPTER SIX

My heart goes to the animals terrified by mankind. Animals are equal to humans. Isn't emotional disturbance the key? An emotional storm leads to abreaction. I want animals to believe in themselves. Stress leads to terror, sometimes fainting, but I want animals *compos mentis*. The *coup de grâce* is fire, which condemns all to flight. I am tempted to round up the customers, cage them and set the zoo alight.

Mid-afternoon, coming down, but still feeling chamicado. I began to sweat terribly. I had found out how to get in the compound of Anita the Giant Anteater. She was lying down, face covered by her tail, which acts as camouflage. Suddenly, I felt a sense of camaraderie, and happiness. The Giant Anteater is emblematic of solitude. A gentle, caring creature, lonely, saintly.

Related in the distant past to the Sloth, who used to stand for human sin, the Giant Anteater is also kin to Armadillos, who spread leprosy. Some can roll into a perfect ball. Others, like the pink fairy, scream for help. Armadillos sleep a lot, like sloths, and obey few rules.

There is a similarity between the elephant and the giant anteater. Both are examples of female leadership, both rear their young devotedly, and visit the dead in touching rituals. Both have evolved to superior life-forms.

Does the Giant Anteater throw light upon co-evolution? The Swedish geek invents some far-fetched process all the way back to whenever. Anteaters were once dwarves, they say. The tongue was only three inches long. Now it is two foot long and can shoot in ants a hundred and forty times a second. The process geek pretends ants were originally eaten one by one, like Maltesers, and their toxicity was infinitesimally small.

A meal now consists of thirty thousand ants a sitting. But there are twenty quadrillion ants, so what does evolution have to say about that? Survival of the fittest? Baloney.

Some still pretend evolution must be slow because changes have to be tiny. They have no idea really. By zooming in on a fiction of merciless competition between ants and ant eaters, they sell fantasies. Yes, there clearly was co-evolution. Perhaps the ants brought about the ant eater.

One example of man's indifference to other creatures is that the Giant Anteater is hunted to death. I love her. I imagine Anita being cornered when young. Somewhat introverted, she would have been wandering along, ignorant of the hurly-burly of the hunters and their perversions. If she made contact with another anteater, she would exchange greetings with delicacy.

Then a horrific attack. A net is thrown over her and when she struggles she is beaten to death. Until molested and attacked by man, she posed no threat. She is, for one thing, toothless; but, like the sloth, has talons which man cuts off or rips away as trophies.

Dalí, the queen of surrealism, much given to boasting and deceit, pretended to have a pet Giant Anteater, and likened her to his guardian angel.

Why are Giant Anteaters victimised?

As the original wormtongue (vermilingua), they were thought to be self-fertilising hermaphrodites by sexually giddy humans, in the early days of Spanish conquest. On first capturing Anteaters, they took them across the Atlantic and presented them at Court in Spain. They claimed the Anteaters' long noses were sexual organs. Men thereafter brutalised these great animals. And still do. I mourn them. When free, like badgers, they are culled by motor cars.

I got close and studied Anita's nose, which is amazing. Man is conditioned to accept, even celebrate, the murder of the Wild. Some cite internecine competition to normalise this necrotic behaviour.

Was it happenstance that led to the theory in Russia which presented symbiogenesis as the explanation of the eukaryotic cell? Was it happenstance that symbiogenesis was excluded from the Modern Synthesis in the West by Selectionists? Is it happenstance that Margulis rescued symbiotic theory just when the destruction of the planet by capitalism was recognised even by scientists? Those who invert the rules, and establish new norms, not infrequently mislead the laity. They inflate death, which they render inevitable, even imperative, in their theories of extinction.

Science has always been a fashion industry. A century of Selection to the exclusion of Symbiosis leaves a legacy of pleonastic theories.

Anita was liable to be burned alive by Impresario dedicated to destroying indigenous people and sacrificing animals to the God of capitalism. Forest fires are prepared years in advance whenever logging and the construction of access roads cause forest degradation and consequently fire. Uncontrolled road building opens the way for undergrowth in a dense biomass which is tinder in the dry season.

Anita's little friends, the ants, also represent death and destruction. Their ancestors were a kind of wasp. Wasps, just like a certain kind of men, will, given half a chance, simulate sex with anything. They have wasted gallons of sperm in the attempt to copulate with orchids.

Flowers mimic insects, particularly the insects' idea of pin-ups as opposed to pin-downs. They send signals to loved-up insect-boys with the kind of pimping entrepreneurialism that makes the human world go round. This is called Pouyannian mimicry.[2]

Co-evolution is a competition in which the wasp or ant is seduced by flowers or by orchids that select wasps for alternative sex. This pseudocopulation is a hate crime to any right-minded wasp with the lofty ambition to metamorph into an ant.

Where does this leave my lovely Anita, Giant Anteater?

"I await my reward," she says. "I once ate two hundred ants' nests in a day. Now I have none. I am lost completely."

Flowering plants and insects interacting appeared in Darwin's *On the Origin of Species*. Plants and insects evolve, it is said, through reciprocal exchanges. Sounds like a dance.

Facing the 'abominable mystery' of how flowers evolved so quickly; co-evolution is suggested as an explanation.[

Pollinators could find flowers by scent and by the snazzy patterns and colours which deceive insects into pseudocopulation.[

When some wasp jumps ship in pursuit of a new life as an ant, it is not thinking about pollination, or sex for that matter.

In the co-evolution of host and parasite, the species with better fitness, it is said, survives. The other party struggles and may pass away. This is known as the Red Queen conundrum, redolent of dark morbidity.

In this race, Death owns the loser, an instructive illustration pointing Westerners to the mortuary.

The cuckoo fits a culture inhabited by Stalin, Hitler, Kennedy, and Philby, who famously command admiration amongst selectionists.

New arrivals improve gene diversity, as does hybridisation.

A few species become highly social, as when sisters surrender breeding duties to the queen, on account of the extraordinarily high degree of relatedness between them. Humans don't fit this bill. This argument has been used to explain apparent altruism and selflessness in ants.

Ants and humans are among the very few 'eusocial' animals capable of building complex societies where groups, each in their specialist roles, co-operate. Commercial companies like Procter and Gamble now source a high proportion of innovation from external networks and companies. At this point, eusocial starts to signify holistic. In some ant species (there are twenty-two thousand species), slavery has become the most productive industry.

But forget altruism. In the distant future my bet is that ants will rule the world. With the demise of Anita, no-one can stop them.

The biggest ant super-colony spans six thousand kilometres, encompassing coastal France, Spain and Italy. But we haven't yet searched hard in Latin America, Asia and Africa. The super-ant in question is Argentinian. The only competent opponent would have to be another ant, capable of breaking the rules of evolution, as a biologist put it, by allowing many queens to reign simultaneously in a super-colony. But don't be fooled. There are no governing rules of Evolution, least of all by a secret protocol of scientists.

As you can see, I am trying to keep up with Evolution, but without success. But the point about ants is a serious one. They are capable of dethroning man. Always look to the environment to explain the direction of travel in Evolution. Global warming is capable of stopping both ants and humans from taking over. But rather than following the dictates of a minor public schoolboy, keep your eyes on the Environment.

I decided to check whether the Chinese Communist Party has the competence of the ant in its leverage/control of the State.

For example, can they devolve leadership across multiple organisations as the Argentinian super-colony does?

If the CCP can do so, maybe we have a basis for coercing humans to respect Nature.

The Nest is proposed as a critical factor in eusocial behaviour, human or ant. I am not sure what a Chinese Communist nest would look like. If we knew, could we devise the equivalent of an anteater to maintain balance of power as the saintly Kissinger would have done. Anteaters enter as many nests as possible, and in a sense so does the CCP, and so must we.

I confess. I am becoming sympathetic to the Chinese Communist Party, as a repository of wisdom. Maybe humanity will compromise on human liberty if they want to get anywhere with global warming.

Deviant behaviour by individual ants is punishable by the Queen, who sometimes puts a chemical marker on the deviant (if, for example, they have laid a naughty forbidden egg). This marker instructs the rank and file to punish the offender. Xi as queen comes to mind. Once again, hats off to the CCP. Their ground-breaking work on brainwashing puts them in a strong competitive position. At this point, I feel I must slap myself on the wrist. I am, after all, falling into Darwin's trap of rationalising everything into the false creode of competition.

To the ant, Anita, though anachronistic, is a Goddess, albeit a dys-social one. They sacrifice themselves to her in great numbers, perhaps dreaming of war against heaven, even martyrdom. It may be that one day an empire of ants will threaten mother earth. Maybe it already does. Is it chance that in each of the countries where rainforests struggle there have been examples of colossal human tyranny, which robs, corrupts and kills without remorse?

Where is the heart of darkness? Who can say? Is it Achebe? Conrad? Mobutu? Or is it the American and French materialists who made Mobutu ever more corrupt? Or is it, belatedly, Xi?

Mobutu built ties with apartheid South Africa, and Israel. He was supported by America, mainly due to his anti-Soviet stance, but also by China as part of Mao's attempts to create a bloc of Afro-Asian nations. The Chinese aid that flowed into Zaire allowed Mobutu to identify as an 'anti-capitalist millionaire'. Ha, ha.

Siberia is another heart of darkness. Who made it so? Solzhenitsyn? Did he not dismantle the Soviet Empire and replace it with dark nationalism, and became a psychopomp to future presidents?

The rainforest, midwife to Ragnarok, dressed in bright flames, will be earth's pall-bearer.

Impenetrably green, hiding in its own shadows, it inseminates its female self, earnestly bringing forth the future man, dire, lethal, irreversible.

The air licks the wet trees. Warm, thirsty, it envelops life, its watery tongue flowing across the Amazonian forest, an anaconda thick, heavy, sluggish, hungry.

On the shores of the Black Sea, fat Silovarchs sun themselves, their mistresses decked out in Tiger skins, servants radiant on the medicine of Tiger bones, bought from Chinese takeaways.

In Mobutu land, the forest is bigger even than Russia's, but is declining metre by metre, as its dwarf elephants and dwarf hippopotami eke out their shortening lifespan.

In Indonesia, not to be outdone, they forget the slaughter of communists, as Palm oil plantations cover their tracks.

In Indochina, communists just slaughtered one another.

What malevolence has been distilled in these dark places? What secretly stews in the curses of ghosts, of cannibals, of the anonymous past? As if the exudations of mankind at their most poisonous have soaked into time itself, oblivious of sanctimony, as the present blames the past, hastening its own end.

Tyrants must have fugitives. Have these fugitives not become proto-species in their own right? Line up the

French Protestants who fled Louis XIV, and do you not discover a tribe at once more civilised and gifted than those they fled. Even the tribe of Fabergé.

Aware that Anita was studying me, I remembered a Giant Anteater once accidentally killed a keeper with its enormous claws, so I moved very gently. But I sensed she was trying to communicate. "I am fed mealworms," she seemed to be saying. "Yuk. There are no termites and no ants. You are not unwelcome, but I do not much like company. The company I crave is a baby. There are no males here. I have no hope of a child."

I felt troubled by this animal, whose natural life had been perverted; but as evolution is believed to have no purpose and no certain destination, planet earth can become the domain of ants to the exclusion of many other life-forms. The demise of anteaters is not unconnected with mankind and is already a fact of life in the rainforests. With no natural predator to stop them, one or more of the current twenty-two thousand ant species will win, possibly by predating on their kind. Then can they, by dint of their social skills, reshape the earth? And as with so many species, Anteaters are already entered in the files of extinct creatures in the realm of entropy.

I believe in God, not the God who accepts animal sacrifice, but the God of all life. The Giant Anteater, wedded to solitude, has about her something holy. She is alone. Saint Paul, once he was converted, never was alone again. The Anteater is, I am certain, one of God's creatures. It would not surprise me to learn she has taken vows. In her are recorded gentleness, altruism, love beyond the ration of many humans.

I love her. In my scales of justice, she outweighs mankind, and does not deserve to die horribly at their hands. I am writing my observations up: call me an outlander. So, too, is the Anteater, a denizen of forest and savannah.

People anthropomorphise a hedgehog called Tiggywinkle, covered in ticks and fleas, because her food supply is buggered and she is so ill the parasites feed on her and multiply. She is the emblem of mother earth sickening as human parasites feed on her.

Let me take a break. The whole package of the Zoo is presented to the world wrapped in schmalz, secrets withheld, information selectively sweetened. It is the opposite of idealism. The decline and fall of Bingo's Zoo is underway.

Bingo announced a change in direction. He has appointed a new Director General of Carnivores. "Now, we will bring the wild unvarnished to our audience," he declared. "No more playing on sentimentality. We will educate." I was mistrustful.

The new man arrived. His name is Underform. He behaves modestly. He has a hole in one of his socks, which I thought a good sign.

"Rainforests, eh?" he said. "What are you doing tomorrow? Come around. I am taking delivery of a young Polar Bear. The wild will be here tomorrow. The terrifying wild."

CHAPTER SEVEN

The next day, I attended the Bear's arrival. Together with Ulysses, I watched spellbound as this long white animal, more like a stoat, save for the vast difference of scale, emerged from a packing case and moved this way and that, nose close to the ground.

Ulysses loves his animals, so they become less afraid. The ones he has a bond with don't self-harm. The monkeys' social grooming shoots up. Loud noises, sudden use of artificial lights and leering strangers threaten. But less so after Ulysses gets to work. Why do humans not show respect? A gifted man like Ulysses does.

Later, I spoke to the new Polar Bear.

"Hello," I said. "Do you have a name?"

"My name is Carnivory. Flesh is my belief. I am the priestess. I perform the sacrifice," she replied.

"Is this not just greed?" I asked. "Why do men invite you into their zoos?"

"Good question. Because mankind is foolish. Because – keep it under your hat – they are half vegetarian and too lazy to acknowledge Carnivory, the supreme life-form on Earth. Our belief comes direct from God. Lack of imagination leads humans to think Polar Bears are the same as them, and therefore will not eat them. Humans believe they can keep Polar Bears imprisoned. Of course, you will not have heard of the great invasion of Russia by Polar Bears in 2019. It failed gloriously. On the day of judgement, killing by us bears will be marked by an infinite supply of sexual rewards."

"So, in the end, Bears will kill all human beings?" I asked.

"Male Polar Bears will. Male Polar Bears will eat the Zoo, lock, stock and barrel, then fornicate in heaven."

"Are they up for it?"

"Two things matter. He who kills, rules. He who rules, kills. You think you can change Nature. But Nature is a chain of slaughter. Healthy nutritious flesh is merely our material joy, but behind it is a deep spiritual force."

"But he who kills is not immortal."

"Who cares? Maybe we will starve. Then we will kill each other."

"Do you have a husband?"

"We are not like that. All male Polar Bears are violent. We females take our lives in our hands to mate. The males dominate our lives and we are grateful. When we give birth, we take the cubs as far away as possible, or the males will eat them. We make dens and even hibernate to protect them. The males would like to subjugate and kill us."

"Then why mate?"

"We are proud of our males. When we come into season, we long hungrily to be inseminated. How we long for that. It is not he who we long for, but it. We are mad with appetite. Mad with longing. All the while we understand suffering and death. This is our answer to the immensity of Fate. Because we welcome life, we are superior. If we have a male cub, we delight in his rage. It guarantees survival, so we teach it. The world is ice, frozen seas, storms, famine. Death, ever present, rules all.

"Your females are not like us. When enough of them have become men, your line will fail."

But though I said nothing, I knew the milk of kindness flows in her veins.

"You humans think you're perfect, but you're not. You have to teach your young for years and years before they can enter the world on safe terms. Even then, they are as predictable as penguins."

"Young humans must be taught," I said. "The ones who do not learn, take to sin."

"Our young survive pain and hardship; with mother's guidance."

Yes, I thought, the mother polar bear is extraordinary, in the love and protection she gives her young. She is passionate, brave, and has endurance beyond any male. And while it is unfashionable to say so, there are many human mothers of the same magnificence.

"The creatures we hunt may change, but we always win," she said. "We never fail our young."

"Have you ever seen a forest?" I asked.

"I have heard of them. I should like my children to."

"Have you seen flowers?"

"We can see colour. Knowledge is survival. In the wastelands, the slightest difference in blues and greys and whites show the path to food and safety. So we escape treachery and death. An ocean of ice, with its floating mountains, groans in awful pain. Whites, blues and greys as far as the eye can see make a landscape of immense meaning. Arctic means Bear. Humans fight to rule in soft and easy places. We rule the cold, hard ones. The Russian, trained to suffering, will endure suffering and terror. But all you humans will flee into our sleeting maws. Come to our northern homeland. Taste our contempt, as under the bleak, unbenighted skies from beneath hell's lakes, rise, through mantle's thaw, the magma of roasting ice which is your fate.

"Global warming threatens you. If ice retreats, we will evolve in other ways, you'll see. We can wait to learn what seals do next and mutate accordingly. Male bears can adopt hibernation, if they should choose, but to do so they must change their feeding habits. They can mate with Grizzlies, opening the door to new food sources. They can migrate to warm climes, in Russia, for example, but again will have to change their feeding habits."

"That appears to be an enormous gamble," I said. "Can Polar Bears not build an Empire under the waves, like whales, or even feast on whales? How teleological would that be? It may take twenty-five million years to grow blow holes, flippers, tail flukes, blubber, submarine eyes, and the capacity to drink sea water. But theories of evolution suggest you might magically mutate by entering the eyes of a thousand needles. We know not how, only that it has been done. The Selectionist geek will map the whales' past history, hoping to prescribe how Polar Bears should match them. Do Selectionists play the Wheel of Fortune?"

How different are Anita and Snow White, I thought. Each endangered, lonely, brave, intensely moral, they have sadly lived their lives on a Manichean Star where Fortune favours those who worship her enough. Snow White will be forced to mate with her Grizzly. Anita will be worshipped by ants everywhere as a mythic death star. Darwin liked to vaunt that cliché 'survival of the fittest'.

I prefer the cliché of transcendent unrewarded service to our planet.

At this point, I begin to see things differently. It is clearly the Environment that evolves, I decided. When the world is suffering, as it now does at the hands of man, Life clings on, desperate to survive in an unreliable environment, desperate to find safety. It's all very well for Darwin to beat time insisting that things change slowly, gradually, in what he saw as a remorseless competition. The Environment can change in seconds. It has extinguished the majority of life-forms on the planet on more than one occasion.

In the Middle Ages, Fortune was respected. It made and unmade us, now growing, now waning, unpredictable like its companion Fate and its emblem the moon above. Now, mankind has grown too important for such simple-minded notions. Clearly, Darwin's vision of progressive change based on competitive superiority explains everything.

And yet... even science, steeped in Darwinism, has unveiled the Earth's catastrophic past.

To me at any rate, Darwin's was a middle-class English worldview. Of course, fitness and natural selection impact survival. But there is no competitive ladder with anthropocentric man on the top rung. The ant is a tiny creature, although the biggest can match a hummingbird in size. Ant species increased in symbiosis with flowering plants. It continues to adapt supremely well to the environment as Fortune and her moronic apprentice, man, shape the planet. But, like all life-forms, their past and their future is a function of external change.

Hitler owed much to Darwin in his conception of an Empire which he planned would survive a thousand years. He set builders to work like ants, but his workers were conquered slaves, of different nationalities. It is almost as if his ambitions sprang out of Darwinian Evolution. As if he was designing a new species. He protected the purity of Germans as of an emerging species. He set them on the road to competitive dominance. He suspended normative behaviour.

He sought to exterminate races and behaviours which in his judgement might obviate Germany, or weaken Germans.

Had he succeeded, he might have actually created a new 'race' by forbidding interbreeding. Darwin would have been vindicated.

The point of this is to illustrate where degenerate Darwinism has misrepresented science. Yet ironically there are many scientists who saw in Darwinism an apotheosis.

Recently, a countervailing thesis suggests itself.

That the Universe contains a myriad of causes (many largely hidden) which may have determined and may determine our planet's future life.

Science has yet to plumb these complexities.

If life-forms on earth are primarily a function of the environment, then our role as curators of the environment has to change, not least in confronting Darwin's loosely conceived notions of extinction and competition.

If, for example, life on earth is not first and foremost the result of competition but of chance which gives rise to speciation and fortuitous survivals in periods of great change, then we must forego the advantage of being an ill-informed curator and assume rigorous and austere self-denial, all on Nature's behalf, to our confessor.

Before we applaud FORTUNA for this breakthrough, let us admit ignorance.

If a life-form changes, and survives those changes, and lasts for millions of years when they are no longer needed, let us hear these histories rather than sanctimonious tales of progress. Changes go on the back burner or lie dormant or hidden for reasons fortunate or fatal. They may slow or obviate adaptation. Physicists live in a fog in which dark energy and dark matter exist unobserved. Physicists are admired and respected. Biology can do better. A planet-wide agenda to save Nature is a duty and a prize. Adaptation is not understood, neither is its timeframe nor its other dimensions. The emergence of very large brains in hominids is a case in point. Darwin would say small, inexorable changes were responsible. But let science consider fortune and fate, and, if they wish, let them trash such inexactitudes and replace them with a new lexicography, not least better terms for ignorance. At this stage, science may treat poetry, religion, and morality as pending.

CHAPTER EIGHT

Ulysses asked me to a meeting with the Sponsor. *Sponsor?* I thought. *Who is that?*

In came Venetsianov.

"I believe you have met His Majesty?"

"Prince!" I greeted him.

He was pleased.

"Since we last met, I have come to a momentous decision. Thanks to America, I can now make funds available to preserve the Rain Forests," he announced... "You will remember I am rather conservative. The Forests are icons of our Russian past. The past is treasure. You British will never save the planet by progressive gimmicks like liberalism, human rights, and identity politics, which trash nation, family, morality and truth. But don't get me wrong. My billions – or at least a billion or two – are available to the cause. And in the light of your work on the Ussuri Tiger, I am appointing you, Mr Heeb, as the Chief Executive."

"May I ask why?"

"For your services to Biodiversity."

"Will you talk to President Xi?"

"I don't think so. I am in regular contact with our Chinese colleagues. Between you and me, I have been promised the Governorship of Oblast Administration, up North. You remember Archangel, where we drove out your troops? I have decided to send Orlik up there."

"Orlik?"

"The Russian name. For Gowler."

"I accept the appointment," I said hastily, quickly recognising the situation was fluid.

"Good, good. The Chinese are excited by our investments in Archangel. And as for your forests, Orlik plans to grow a whole new rainforest as global warming advances North."

"I am conversant with a number of wild animals in the region, notably Polar Bears," I replied. "If you agree, I would like to appoint a truly charismatic woman as my number two? Someone expert in the Biome."

"Don't overcomplicate," said Venetsianov, sucking his teeth. "OK, then. Maybe someone like Eleniya, eh? We Russians are much loved in the rainforest world. In India, there are many still attached to Tolstoy, the champion of the peasants. Neither Marx nor Lenin quite got that right. Brazil hasn't, either. Blair and Bush lied. Their misjudgement laddered the stocking of international law. We Russians opposed them in good faith. We are the last bastion against the ruthless West. Tolstoy, remember, was an anarchist and saw governments as corrupt, not least the democracies. The axis between Russia and India conceals an enormous truth which will shape the world. Orthodox

Christianity, Buddhism, and Hinduism, not democracy, will mobilise the poor, the peasants, the downtrodden, and without the millstones of Marxism, the Vatican or American-style capitalism.

"We will tackle global disaster by co-operation, free of violence and corruption."

"Do you accept totalitarianism, though, Prince?"

"I am, to be frank, insulted by such a question. We Russians are Christians. We are heirs to Byzantium and Ancient Greece. Driven by intellect, worship, art, not atheism, we owe our ideas to Aristotle. Our Black Sea, our Crimea, were Greek colonies. Great civilisation is our legacy. Our Patriarch leads spiritual rebirth.

"As a Prince, I love all my subjects. Like Tolstoy, I will dress as a peasant. Many, many poor and helpless people were murdered by the revolution. The whole idea of revolution is to be first to seize power and the last to cede it. In short, dictatorship of the seditious and the odious.

"Seditious revolutions bring *bêtes noires*. Peasants become cannon fodder, to be continuously killed by Marxists, and then disposed of as carrion."

Venetsianov was shaking now. "Stalin," he said, "was a Georgian, poor man, a cipher, coined by these marxists."

"You lay bare humanity," I said. "To despise and murder the weak is not exclusively marxist. America has led the way in economic and territorial expansion at the expense of Nature itself. I believe mankind may yet be extirpated and God may have to start over. First, let us free the animals."

"And how is that to be done?"

"By revolution."

"Not another one!"

"The French chose terror as their revolutionary weapon of choice. The Marxists copied them. Christ speaks for those they terrorised and killed."

Venetsianov, trembling and exhausted, said repeatedly, "Tolstoy stood for Christianity and Anarchy", as if this motto was relevant.

"Freedom is money, Prince," I said.

"Manipulation of the many by the few?" he retorted. "Eton continues to produce élitist Prime Ministers and Chancellors, while pretending democracy. In America, votes are monetised and the rich oppress the poor. If you are to save the Rainforests, the majority of animals and humans in them must benefit.

"And yet I see where you are going with this. Our naval power will control the Arctic passage to the East. We will make a fortune, and reforge the Franco-Russian pact. A charismatic woman might help," he said.

"Once financially strong," he said, "you Brits came under pressure when you were no longer able to vouchsafe the global system. The Americans reshaped the world in their own unwholesome image."

I must think, I thought. War was weighing on my mind. The impact of nuclear war on global warming. I put it to him: "Great powers contemplate nuclear war once again. Is that good?"

"Naturally," he said.

CHAPTER NINE

So I formed a Save the Rain Forest Group and debriefed them.

There are five people in the team: Annie does aquatic mammals. She is too clever by half.

Circe, an expert in biodiversity, tells tragic tales to the City. 'Get inside their heads' is her motto.

Snag calls this rubbish. A tough egg, he worked for Venetsianov, but was let go. He wants forceful strategies, yet there is depression behind his outbursts.

We have a temporary member, called the Major. Circe flirtatiously calls him Sausage. Very nice man, plump, modest, fastidious. Behind his bland features lie family mishaps, deprivation, and shame. He has a golden asset: his dog Bite, an alter ego, who sleeps in his bed.

Staying in a B and B in Kent, I had an appointment to see a junior Minister in London. I chose to drive up, but my car broke down in the hills south of Faversham, where the lanes can lead nowhere. There were no houses nearby, so I gave up all hope of making it. At that moment, a small bug-eyed sports car appeared. In it sat the Major with his dog. I was unimpressed. He looked surprised.

"Rung the AA, then?" he asked.

"Are we far from Faversham?"

To cut a long story short, he arranged to have my car fixed in jig time.

I don't know why, but I found him calm and his generosity extraordinary. It was rendered in an unassuming manner. I invited him to join the team.

They ranged around the table, leaning forward expectantly. "The Russian forest is not that different to the Amazon," I said. "These are desperate countries. Big rainforests in countries impoverished and corrupt. The world must change if we are ever to extract ourselves from Shit Street.

"Rainforests are ecosystems with layer after layer of species, interacting and supporting one another. Remove a layer and, like Takeradi bricks, they collapse."

"Colonialism," said Snag. "Brazil is the last great colonial power, egging on its conquistadors to colonise and loot the forests, and the indigenous people."

"Kent used to be forest," said Annie. "Eighty percent of Germany was forest. Then the Germans chopped it down. They made rafts of interlocking trees; sent them down to Holland, who made ships, sailed to Brazil, imported slaves, and created vast plantations. What comes around goes around. The Dutch got kicked out by the Portuguese."

"The problem," I said, "is not least the loss of biodiversity. But if COP promises are not met, we are all toast."

"Come off it," said Snag. "Be careful not to write off technology."

I cut him short. "Humans are failing the rainforests, and six thousand species face extinction. Animal populations are on average half the size they were. Rainfall is declining. Forests are morphing into savannah.

"Farmland is tanking around the world and this is leading to wholesale degradation. Weather systems are depressing food production.

"Desertification and flooding are gathering momentum.

"These are things the West can't solve on their own… To get China, India, Brazil on side, all must see past colonialism and pull their weight."

"If I was India," said Snag, "I'd drive a hard bargain. In view of the past, India is the lynchpin. It has been colonised for ever. Turkic, Afghanistan Mongol, Indo-Europeans?"

Annie then went full tilt. "Russia, China, India, all use a different order of coercion to make things happen. They are our only hope, not America, which slides into senility."

That word coercion once again.

"So?" I said.

"Unlike us, China endured vast death tolls to reach their goals. Facing disaster, they concentrate on survivors, not casualties."

"What could we subcontract to them?"

"When you endure death and suffering on that scale, you think differently. At the birthing of China, the waters broke and the Yellow River carried all before it. Crisis after crisis of lethal flooding hewed out the Chinese character long, long before Marx or Mao.

"Faced with humanity's extinction, the Chinese find solutions which the West, trapped in individual liberties, cannot," said Annie. She was never going to climb down on this one.

The others turned on her. "We have centuries of political progress compared with China. Their nationalism is like Hitler's. Don't come the madam, madam," growled Snag.

"Anyway, what has this to do with Rainforests?" demanded Circe.

"I probably sound fascist," said Annie, "but we have to change."

Everyone fell silent.

"I'm not so sure about coercion," I said. "I can promise new rainforests in Russia and Canada. If democracies could plan long-term, then even more. Be practical. We need less folk tales, less folk medicine, more investment. So much depends on wresting money from the West, short-sighted and corrupt though they may be. India, Russia, China must do the heavy lifting."

"What about pharma?"

"Look at Brazil. There are four hundred animals used for medicine in the Amazonian forests. Take the supernatural Jaguar, whose teeth, skin and bones are used in Chinese medicine. Take the Cayman. It is eaten for lunch in the Amazon, its teeth, skin, fat, and penis used as medicines for snake bite, asthma, stroke, bronchitis, backache, rheumatism, thrombosis. See? Magic. Or take the Armadillo: its tail and skin are used for earache and asthma. Lizards are aphrodisiacs."

"So hocus pocus magic will save Nature?" said Snag, and his face looked crocodilian.

"Not magic, but revolution," I suggested. "What we have to get our heads around is ignorance. Take the yam. It has travelled to the rainforests in Papua, Melanesia, to Amazonia, supplementing man's foraging, not displacing rainforests. We need a passionate ideology and a whole new understanding of forestry."

"To order? No chance."

"There are umpteen plants with incredible medicinal value. The Wasai tree, which wears a scarlet skirt of roots and cleanses your kidneys. The Lapacho, with anti-cancer properties. The Sodo plant, that cures addictions.

"My view of humankind is that in the ideasphere they swarm like locusts into incoherent emotion. They protect outdated beliefs in Darwinism."

"No evidence of Metamorphosis," said Snag. "Communism. Fascism. 1984. Each of its time. But no evidence that humans change to order."

"The French Revolution?"

"Came packed with lies. The French, the American, the Russian revolutions – each lied, hid greed, pretended idealism. They lied."

"You can't sanitise revolution," Annie argued. "If we want Utopia, enforce it. Every week, archaeology discovers places where man worked the forests. For up to fifty thousand years they planted in and round the forest, not against it. Back to the drawing board."

"We don't have time," said the Major.

"In Cambodia, they built a conurbation, connected to jungle, with well-drained fields, and canals, interspersed with fish lakes. It can be done," I said.

"Let the Brazilians get on with it then."

"Beliefs AND modern science are the tools we have. AND revolution.

"Microbes in every one of us outnumber our genes. The microbes in our guts are the little MI5 guys that steer health, immunity, diet, cravings. The biome of the whole forest is unimaginable.

"Let's work on that.

"I need money, money, money. A Money Forest… People love animals. Even FTSE 100 Chairmen do. Switch the donors onto the fragility of life; highlight extinctions. My idea is to make the Rainforests into locomotives, pulling weather, health, chemistry, and spirituality along."

"No point exaggerating," said Snag.

"You mean tap into religion?" Annie asked. "As an atheist, I object, full stop."

So I had to row back a little. I tried to explain. "In my world, each clan had a totem, who protected them. They felt this unity, which joins men, animals, trees with the land they share."

"Sounds like socialism," said Snag.

"It's still alive in the Amazon, in Guyana."

"Take your word for it," said the Major.

Circe agrees to spend some time with a tribe in Guyana. Venetsianov is funding her.

Everyone was delighted.

CHAPTER TEN

Annie, my right-hand man, observes that small-bodied animals with fast metabolisms live more intensely than large animals with slow metabolic rates. By large animals, I think she means Gowler, aka Orlik, who, instructed by the Prince, came and talked to us about Russia.

Here was a chance to observe an alpha male, warts and all.

He disappoints me.

"The firefly experiences time more slowly than us. Small animals use time to regulate behaviour in ways beyond us," he said.

"House mice rely on proteins in their urine to sniff out and avoid mating with blood relatives, thus avoiding incest. We relied on God to message a similar instruction. Mice regulate themselves."

I chime in. "The Selectionist will pounce. In many species, they say, one sex, usually the female, leaves the group at adolescence. That way they can't mate with their own family. *Selection, you see?* they say. Where does this leave God?"

"Exactly," said Annie, delighted.

"We have to digest His previous messages," I replied.

"Evolution is hard to understand," said Gowler. "Sauropods got big and long – a hundred and twenty tonnes, I think, and a hundred foot long. You have to ask yourself, can such an evolutionary process be of any utility whatsoever? If Nature's processes are so inefficient, then forget Nature; empower man."

"This sounds like hubris," said Annie.

Gowler glared. His alpha tendencies lead him to assume that she plays no part in setting our agenda. Engagement, courtship, deference are foreign to him.

I injected some humour.

"When you get that big," I remarked, "the digestive system yields benefits of scale? They farted so much back then, they and planet earth combusted. Which explains why therapods evolved in the opposite direction into little birds."

Annie laughed more than necessary.

"I believe we should congratulate you on your recent promotion to supervise the Forests in North Russia," I said unctuously.

"That is premature," he said sharply.

I noticed my group disengaging. Not only that, but they wanted to subordinate themselves as though they took pleasure in submission to him, of all people.

"The forests are the richest domain of biodiversity," he said grandiloquently.

"Humans destroy forest life, trees, fungus, animals," I interjected. "They enslave and eat animals on a stupendous scale. No platforming has failed to abolish anything.

Mankind enslaves itself, especially women. Only revolution will do."

"Leave that to experts," he glowered.

"What do scientists see when they map the genome? Not poetry, music or religion, or even empathy (things they have not mastered)."

This brought proceedings to a halt. Later, my little group regrouped and discussed events.

The Major was thoughtful. "Does the current meme of evolution explain biodiversity or symbiosis?" he asked. "In the forest, vast numbers of creatures cohabit and share. Many fruit trees disperse their seeds through animals, birds, even fungi.

"Distribution depends on these specialist third parties who plant the seeds in virgin territories, where plantings thrive without much competition. If one such specialist distributor goes extinct, it may be curtains for the seed producer. In other words, one species going extinct threatens the others. Do we understand the synergy between species? Does Orlik, when he plans new forests? Does the Apple watch measure our extinction?

"I have set up shop in the Zoo. Let's use that opportunity to build a bridgehead in the rainforests. What did I learn about Russian forests?

"The forest as ocean in which all life is inlaid." I was morphing into someone else. In Russia, I had taken drugs on the precipice of a failing world.

I set off in search of trees to worship.

Annie describes the scene.

Diary. Tuesday 11 May

Went for walk with Heeb. The road climbs beneath high banks. Trees lean gothically over us.

The vault colourless above save for branches, serpentine, wooden ogees which exercise the eye, offering glimpses of distant fields in silent paradise. And when the hill is climbed, long vistas of countryside roll beneath us, downs washed by a green discoloured brush drenched in rains minutes past, and above, heavens dilute in faded grey.

Pure Annie.

A month went by. We met in Chiswick.

"The TV is a cliché about the Wild. Nice series, stunning production values, no real feeling. No empathy because no belief amongst viewers. *The Iliad*, Shelley, Blake, Pound, Yeats, Eliot. All judged great," said Annie. "But all failed the rainforest."

"Oh, poetry? What about the Wordsworths?"

"All sensibility," she replied, "and sugar, cotton wool and fluttering spirit, presences sublime that disturb, but do not kill. Nature never betrayed the human heart, nor vice versa.

"Only Hermetic Vaughan, a Welshman, knew Nature," she said despondently.

"Attenborough?"

"Dear Attenborough. Not a poet."

"Wordsworth does not pass muster."

"No, no," cries Annie anew. "The Germans. They had their feet on the ground: Schelling, Fichte, put Nature before man. Novalis said human beings come to know themselves enlivening nature.

"The reason I signed up to save the Rainforest is the idea of salvation," she cried. Perspiration shone on her lovely face.

She thinks I am interesting. She is for ever asking about South America. She took time off to show me her mother's garden in Suburbia.

"These are Brugmansias," she said.

"Of course," I replied "Glorious flowers like trumpets blew across the Andes. These no longer exist out in the Wild. More beautiful than any other flower."

"Why did they disappear?" she asked.

"Some say a wild animal, now extinct, was their agent, eating and spreading seeds in season. Then under attack by some predator, this unknown middleman, was driven to extinction… Perhaps."

"So, in the wild, Brugmansias ceased. A Rainforest in microcosm?"

"They say the creature that spread it was driven to death by something ancient. Do you credit that?"

"Gomphotheres?"

"Whatever. Or perhaps the new kid on the block. Jaguars are known to feed on hallucinogenic stuff?"

"The yage? *Banisteriopsis caapi*?" Annie always knew more than me. And regularly put me in my place.

"Did the Jaguar in the Andes lose touch with its own reality?" she asked.

"Jaguars are magical, like the rainforest itself."

"Eating *Brugmansia arborea* for an incredible high? Its armiger, that glorious flower, its angelic tuba, never went extinct. Thanks to my Mum."

"Andean priests," I said, "smoked the leaves to see the future. I have drunk Chicha and it blew my mind. Shamans, helped by magic mushrooms, talk to ancestors."

"What a wonderful life you've lived. I do so envy you," she said.

"Take a warm bath, then wander round the house totally wet with the heating going full blast. That's humidity.

"Crane your neck. Look up. Trees like the Sumaumeira as high as Nelson's Column. Lianas, entwined around tree trunks, passion flowers, green and blue, red, and yellow. Red monkey brushes. In the understory, the brilliant red achiote, orchids and the landing lights of red bracts that welcome in the hummingbirds. Look up again and see the majestic kapok, one hundred and fifty foot high, the tree of a thousand coffins. And see the groves of banana, palm, rubber beside the cacao, evergreen, glossy, oblong, drooping bright green leaves. Brush away the swarms of midges and look up at those elongated pods, bright yellow, some deep purple, numerous ridges along its length. And if you dare go that far, watch the little boys clamber the palms for their delicious fruit."

***

Annie's mum regards me as beyond the pale. A stupid woman with much money, her brain small, achieving nothing save golf, Wimbledon, social engagements. Spoils Annie, buying expensive clothes the like of which no-one can afford.

I tutor Annie in other things.

"Never take Brugmansia as a drug, although smoking the dried leaves does little harm. Best left for the locals closest to Nature. The intoxication's so intense you can neither see nor hear. Once chamicado, you go mad, or get robbed. If the Garden of Eden was shared by men and animals, maybe they got high together."

"You are right," said Anne, her big brown eyes welling with tears. "Who needs poetry, then? All that iridescent verse? The past as it goes extinct makes our world shabby."

"I have this foreboding," I replied.

Even then, Annie struck me as a child. Her parents heartily disliked each other. Rumour has it that they open their garden to the village, and stand back to back, welcoming their respective friends and exchanging never a word between the two of them. Annie sides with her mother and in some odd way looks up to her. No criticism is allowed. As a consequence, mummy spoils her rotten. So Annie survives as a sort of hybrid; a bit of her is masculine, but most is mother. One consequence is that she is absolutely atheist, her father being a church warden. I suppose Annie inherits poetry and sensibility from some ancient forebear. I noted in the early days of our relationship she believes in power, her admiration for me as project leader, my insistence on good order, further clues. What else did Annie inherit from her father? Drink? Misogyny? Not her unshakeable belief in the superiority of her sex.

What I have in common with her is the sights and sounds of Nature.

Walking through the English woods, I compare them with the Russian Forest and feel I have gone deaf. Then I hear trees whispering, sap retreating, the hush of sanctity inhaled, spirits withdrawn into mystery.

I follow tiny shards of sound dissolving into silence; and then a rushing back as if life is flooding into every twig and stamen.

English Forests are to my ears a tweed of coloured noise, barely audible. The clicks and ticks that weave in and out of leaf and bough make silence beautiful, painting it with tiny notes of music. Compare the silence of a field of rape, in which all insect life has died at the hands of the anaerobic farmer.

Suddenly, like a brushful of lapis, a blackbird sings, turning the woodland into symphony.

The past holds the answers. Woods are where spirits dwell. I listen for them. Here, light, pure and white, enters the landscape, dispersing through the greenwood, shining holy. In the evening, the last birdsong drains away, and we feel the apocalypse of sylvan night. My own people are closer to the stars. Magic holds sway.

Anne was poetising. At the feet of the most luminous trees, she sang. I see worshippers, humus, vast networking fungi, living acolytes, the ghosts of aconites killed by poison; mouse bane, leopards' bane, women's bane. The sweet and sour scent of pine needles.

We share this experience in the woods? It reveals the brotherhood of root, the bas reliefs of leaf, the tattoos of ivy, the orange rusts of ochre. Grey powders of mildew swirl, animating Spring. In short, a canopy of angels.

Like oracles, like Sybils, they call out. We forbid them, we stifle their cries. We fail to hear their prayers. Those swaying trees face the wind, tensing against humans who besiege them. At last, she fell silent. Annie is right, of course. It is impossible to weigh mankind against Nature. If you do, Nature instantly is lost.

Snag is the nearest thing to a Mr Fixit in the team, always trying to prove himself. An upright, middle-class man, very active, he offered to take me on a nature ramble, to get to know each other better. He passed on his observations of badger setts and fox dens.

Small beer compared with Russia.

"I was going to say," he replied. "I was brought up in Rhodesia, you know. Elephant makes lion small."

I gather Snag was in the habit of looking after a terrier for the local hunt. He saw a snobbish status in being a follower.

"What does it involve?" I asked.

"We dig Charlie out. An opportunity to put the terriers to work."

"Don't foxes have litters about now?"

"No. Back in March," he replied. "We get cubbing in August, when young foxes meet a hound for the first time. They can't believe their eyes. They run about, bumping into one another and running headlong into trees as if they're blind."

"I hear the followers are girls."

This did not seem to please him.

"They're obsessed with horses," he said, "but not too keen on blood. I saw one blooded once. She shrieked."

"So the men are at the sharp end," I said. At that moment, I was thinking of Eleniya.

"We're all animals," he remarked dolefully.

"How so?"

"Testosterone works its magic, not least in mammals. Just watch the Elephants. When they get into musth, their testosterone goes up a hundredfold. They'll attack anything that gets between them and love. It makes me laugh, people talking about animal rights. Animals have no moral sense."

"You mean like Orlik?"

I changed the subject. "You don't see too many girls in the old hunting prints. The gender gap narrowing?"

"The hilltops are held by men. Engineers, Mathematicians, apex."

"Not what I hear."

"Engineers who turn terrorist. Men."

"Where are you going with this?"

"Men are men. We map the world. We court risk. We study process. We invent, we lead. Cromwell, Newton, Erasmus. Men who ordered life. We go to war if called upon. If we refuse, we provoke extinction. I'm on your side. If things get rough, call on me. Badgers are apex, yet subsist on worms. They slaughter hedgehogs. The people carrying placards pretend three billion humans don't kill fifty billion chickens every year, and cruelly."

"Man not superior, then?"

"That's not what I said. Man has humour and philosophy, but deceives, exploits, misleads."

"What about your dog?"

"Oh. He has a sense of humour."

"And his idea of a joke is…?"

"Rolls in carrion, then wags his tail."

"Masking his smell so he can kill?"

"Dogs roll in fox poo, then smell dangerous. What's your point?"

"Foxes eat dogs' turds as a source of nutrition," he adds earnestly. Their diet is that bad."

"Famine?"

"Not in England. Not in May."

"Let's make the most of it."

"Yes. This is England. White blossom; white flowers. White Campion," I said.

"Wood Anemone, Cow Parsley, Oxeye Daisies," he added. "May, when wrens make nests. Did you know, the male makes up to six nests, and if he's lucky, a female chooses just one of them. Lucky humans don't waste energy like that."

"Isn't May yellow?"

"Bees love it. Dandelions. Bullfinch chew the seed. Goldfinch love it, too; siskin, blackbird, bumblebee, sparrow, butterfly."

Snag seemed excited.

"White for me," he said. "I'll take you up the park and show you. There is an orchid there called the poached egg plant. Takes eight years to come to flower with a little yellow lip you hardly see because it's hidden. The ovary is the flower's stalk growing out of patches of bare chalky soil beneath the beeches. It is blessed with the most beautiful white flower. So elegant, it is to die for."

"This doesn't sound like you. I took you for a hard no-nonsense man."

"There's bishop weed, like lace; and I've heard a ghost orchid has been sighted there. No leaves, and can only flower with the help of Fungi."

"Ah, symbiosis in old England?"

"But the moths are even better," he said. "Have you ever seen an elephant hawk moth? I'm sure they're immigrants from Africa. Children of the sphinx decked out in gold and pink, they look like little elephants with tusks of white. And in September, the caterpillars feed on willow herbs and frighten the birds with huge dark eyes."

"What birds?"

Redstarts, warblers, nightingales, martins, cuckoos, all in decline."

He wasn't such a bad chap.

We walked on. Light shone down upon apple blossom. The little apple trees wound about the stakes, enticing them like columbines.

Nature suddenly seemed healthy. The rainforests will survive and boom.

I treat Annie, as my number two. "Venetsianov makes me laugh," I said. "He thinks you're beautiful."

She blushes. "I don't care what he thinks." (Meaning, what's your opinion?)

"We must raise more money. Outgoings are running ahead of income."

"You sound like dad."

"You're innocent in the ways of the world, Annie."

"The problem is that Rainforests have no salience," she replied. "For most people, their disappearance is below the eyeline. We prefer fairy stories to reality. I'll tell you what we need. Creativity. There is a lady I'd like you to meet. She has written a book on it."

Annie's creative lady looked like Elizabeth I. Ageing, crowned with hair not red but black. A last great Maiden lady before maidens lose their heads. She spoke with hauteur.

"You a student?" she demanded.

"Of Rainforests. Did Annie not say?"

"A soap salesman pioneering palm oil? Lever bought vast acres in the Congo."

"And created soap?"

"I enlisted mothers in the battle against germs. I used his soap to fight the battle. Was your mother gentle, caring, house proud, in the struggle against dirt?"

"Sounds unAmerican."

"Our ads were subtle. We wove magic spells and invoked archetypes. Only the ignorant disrespect the past."

"Darwin?"

Her face went red with indignation.

"Never mind all that. Your job is to conjure the wild."

"The wild seems, well, inhuman."

"Then change it. Truth lies hidden in the human mind. Unearth it."

"Who is to say?"

"Humanity ever inches towards the unnatural," she replied. "America will not keep the East quiet for long. Revive nature or watch it die."

"Do archetypes connect with the young? Really?"

"Advertising wins elections."

"Britain, once a world leader in chemicals, cars, shipyards, computers, now depends on advertising?"

"Don't underestimate creativity," she snapped. "Harold Wilson crammed together disparate motor companies, under one roof, believing this created scale. His sort of socialism assumed Governments dictate what people want. Even the Chinese don't do that. Symbiosis. There lies the path into your Forest."

She was, I thought, soft in the head.

Back home, I thought about the Royal Society. Darwin was not my idea of science. He imagined change.

A few highly selective threadbare facts. No-one had heard of punctuated equilibria. He wanted to account for tiny accruals, few of them audited.

Darwin's theory made extinction necessary. Blame Malthus, who justified extermination. Darwin translated this to mean that failing species go extinct, although when he lost concentration he, too, used the word extermination. In the wider culture, the idea of extinction becomes sanctimonious. The working class must adapt! Nature must take care of itself! Most of all, it sanctifies shrugging shoulders, accepting extinction as inevitable, beyond the agency of man.

And where does that get us? We have no more idea of the origins of life than Aristotle did, and less resolve than Mao to protect it. Dinosaurs preceded us, so diverse, so strange, ultimately so transient. When an asteroid hit them, the atmosphere was methane, and instantly caught fire. What did Darwin's account add up to? What have the Darwinistas to say? They can't even agree what they don't know. Lead thinkers, hungry to disrupt some old religious straw man, do little to save biodiversity. Disruption is not particularly welcomed in the learned journals, where copycats are more the rage. Take farming. Farmers seek subventions. State capitalism subsidises farming. Tax payers make farmers rich; some increase their scale of operations. Big, rich farmers produce high-carbon livestock, and some over-use pesticides. Nature is the casualty.

Darwin thought his version of evolution would optimise man's ethical potential.

He attached importance to natural selection. Finches and the size and shape of beaks and feet became a favoured illustration.

Did one species arrive in the Galapagos and become many? Facing little or no competition, did the Finches spread round the islands, finding niches in which new variants of beak size, and shape, could flourish? (Adaptive radiation.) Did they increase variability through genetic flows like hybridisation? Calmoduline, a protein coding gene, helped beaks change. Variation between epigenetic genes helped birds adapt to different diets. Extinction was not a significant factor, on the evidence available.

Natural selection, gradual and slow, was Darwin's gig. Other forces were at work. A species pump is explored. Archipelagoes of thousands of islands during periods of rising sea levels shrank available territory, in some cases, for example, to six or seven big islands. This raises questions about isolation and reconnection. On an isolated island, sex may be more important in selection. Changes in ecology lead to reconnection and increased diversification. Change in climate even more so.

If a plethora of new species hit the ground simultaneously, evolution itself will likely evolve. In the case of the Galapagos, the finches, it is argued, found fourteen niches largely unoccupied. Natural selection was granted a public holiday. Variations on a beak was top of the pops.

The wheel turns. Humans are degrading the Galapagos, whose finches are forecast to go extinct. A parasitic fly which lays larva in their nests is attacking nestlings. Did Darwin foresee the demise of Nature at the hands of man? Did he consider that the finches may have arrived with a full range of beak shapes and sizes acquired and stored over millions of years, and if so, what further basic research is necessary to stabilise threatened ecosystems?

The Major is making headway in his love for Circe. Suddenly, he breaks cover.

I don't like to make a song and dance, but Physics was my subject. It has moved on. The new Physics says: once two particles have become entangled, then... they are no longer different objects.

How true, I think, if you're in love. The Major has elided with Circe.

My twin and I are one. Raised apart. How similar we are. Same food – we share a taste for snakes – same passion to protect forests; same interest in visiting zoos. Our favourite colour is green, our instinct is to worship God. Our love of drugs and magic. Evolution synchronised.

Darwin divided evolution into adaptation or extinction. Until recently, the death rate of human babies was catastrophic, yet women fell pregnant again and again, despite the consequences. In the wild, carnivores snack upon the very young of any species. Survival so often depends upon the mother. Not the choice 'twixt fight or flight, but of oxytocin and maternal hormones which can determine nutrition, concealment, affiliation and therefore survival. The phenotype can be determined by the environment. The genotype can be influenced by the environment and the genotype of the mother, evidenced by the mother supplying messenger RNA or proteins to the egg, sometimes controlling the size, sex or behaviour. This phenotypic plasticity, e.g. response to environmental change such as acclimatisation (much still to be learned) and learning from womb to death.

Darwin failed to give motherhood its due. Some, influenced by fellow travellers, can value sexual freedom at the expense of motherhood. But through the perspective of survivability and natural selection, motherhood is the determinant of survival. Confucius saw family as a cornerstone of morality. Revolution is overdue if mankind is to improve survivability of species in neoteny. Put a price on this. The price must be high, to reflect biodiversity, the treasure of the earth. Debit the price on the public purse. Spend on childcare and early education, supervised only by women. Evolution is not a competitive sport between boys. I thought of Adele, my penguin girl. Ulysses diagnosed Zoochosis, by which he means the misery of her incarceration.

Annie has written a poem. Here it is.

> Did once the holy spirit come
> into the woods and into leaf?
> I search for clues.
> This bright electric amber gum?

> This beetle, ticking as it chews
> each yellow rotten oaken crumb?
> Beneath the leaves of gilded hues
> shrews listen for the rabbits' drum,
> watch green girls milking honeydews,
> hear sap rise through wooden flues.
> Some deem a tree to be their muse.
> Leaf-miners, grubs, worms, thrips benumb
> the birds for choice. Fungi cruise
> forest roots. Spiders aerially plumb
> for insects, threading silk through sunlit dews.
> So care for wildwoods, or succumb
> to the nightly spirits. Pontiffs refuse
> to let their Gods run wild. I strum
> God's song upon the wind to make you lose
> your mind. I am Tom Thumb,
> by day invisible, by night unseen. So choose.
> Love the wild or stay away and pray.
> Lest Dawn should never come.

"How do you envisage using this poetry?" I asked.

She blushed. "I was just trying to put into words what you teach us," she explained.

"It certainly sidesteps the Ussuri Tiger."

She looked devastated. "I knew you wouldn't like it."

"Who is Tom Thumb?" I asked. "Do you need to kill him?"

"No shit," she said and guffawed.

Why did she send me this poem? Was it intended to be a sort of private link between us?

I thought more and more about falling in love. As a Tree Spirit, I am attracted to trees, to animals and to humans. This gives me insights others do not have. I see no reason why I may not pursue opportunities with all three. My ideal human lover is female, left-handed and red-haired. There are health risks associated with each; but red hair comes top. It seems to be linked to passion, anger, and creativity. Sadly, Annie is dark; Circe has a dash of ginger about her.

"Would you dye your black hair red?" I asked Annie.

"I would not. Red is for losers. Once, it was a sign of greatness and divinity. Achilles, Helen, Aphrodite. The ancient Gauls and the Caledonians. It would not have surprised the Druids to be told that the future of Europe was red heads. Imagine Europe dominated by them. Imagine them as a new species. Instead, Fortune shone on Caesar, and the redheads, once powerful, were crushed and their descendants sold into slavery. The story of evolution told by Rossetti and Caravaggio."

How sad. I crave the love of left-handed ginger women, both in decline.

This did not go down well with Annie. When in Rome, she says, you should adapt to English girls.

"Like the understated English countryside? Astonishingly beautiful? Could be addictive."

"You're learning," she said.

I told her about my research into the Baboon enclosure.

"It sounds as if it pays the alpha male to create mayhem. That juices up the hormones."

"So he will get yet even more alpha," she suggested. "Think of Stalin. He kept disrupting systems, people, geography, and in so doing became impregnable, an autocrat who killed to extend ascendancy."

"The party supported him?"

"The alpha system relies on mutual networks. Depends on how you define alpha. The oppressed are conditioned to support the bosses.

"In early times in Northern Europe, tribes generally at war had to find and to retain great leaders. A tribe without a leader risked extinction. Once invited, he took over. Would you call that democracy?"

"No."

"Is it consistent with any other species?"

"Possibly."

"Does it have advantages?"

"Loyalty?"

"Perhaps. Freedom to call the shots. One drawback: if he fails, you must get rid of him."

"I see."

At this point, the wider world kicked in. Venetsianov's secretary sent me the card of a man called Kwong. Apparently, he has a Panda to sell. I was expected to deal with him, since Giant Pandas live in Rainforests.

When I met him, I said, "Don't Pandas just eat bamboo? I mean in China? And bamboo is a kind of grass, so they are not forests at all, are they? Maybe I'm the wrong man to speak to?"

He looked impassive. He was beautifully dressed and had the most exquisite things made of gold: a lighter, a cigarette case, a watch and two pens.

"Do you want to buy my Panda?" he said, as if I was a time-waster.

"You need to talk to Bingo."

"Not available."

"He has the money," I explained. "I am responsible for soft power and rainforests. What dietary arrangements would we need to make?"

"I can supply you with bamboo."

"Nothing else?"

"It evolved to eat bamboo."

He took out a small mirror and examined his hair, which was lustrous, black.

"Soft power," he said. "You know Tao? Earth is reflection of heaven?"

"I believe so. Who said that?"

"Kwang Tang-te."

"Same name…?"

"No, no, no," he said angrily. "My name Kwong. Not Kwang. Tao First Causes is mother of the World. Nature is the effect of Tao. My Panda perfect. Not like extinct Bulgarian. You want buy?"

"I don't understand Tao."

"No matter. Christianity already popular in China. Tao and Christianity partners, isn't it? Islam says nature is reflection of men's souls. Men's souls are corrupt. They corrupt nature. This Panda not corrupt; can come sale or return," he said, licking his gold pen.

Pocketing his card, I agreed to correspond on matters of interest.

He said, "You are a good man. Who does not love Panda has no soul."

Later, I had a party with members of my group. An unseasonable BBQ and sing-songs. Annie brought a handsome man. I could tell he was gay. Circe brought a woman with two red-faced children, aged nine or ten. They shrieked and cried and pulled each other's hair. Major Sausage, who did not seem to have relatives or friends, made up for this by bringing eats: cocktail food; sprays of sugary pink confections, the kind you might find on a knickerbocker glory; and some tandoori chicken. Snag, like a tribal elder, came with an amalgam of children and old people, none related to one another. When these people were not arguing, they appeared to be bipolar, now happy, now withdrawn. The overriding impression was that the English are a rich store of emotional confusion.

Meanwhile, I was determined to do more research in the Zoo. I took a little flat nearby. I was energised. My first night I slept well and woke exhilarated. It seems I am the only one to notice, but the sound of a Zoo is a symphony sounding notes of love, of hope, of fear, the cry of peacocks, the boom of the Siamang. Sounds musical, yet microtonally unexpected, juxtaposed to astonishing dissonance.

Zoos began as vanity projects. Rulers like Alexander the Great expected animal sacrifice. Umble, entrails, the ambrosia of hungry predators, were served up in modest portions to the gods, the rest hogged down by men. Weirdly, they wanted the animal to be willing. Some gods, satisfied by beheadings, amputations, holocausts, demanded the sacrificial animal be decked with garlands. As you can imagine, Zoos were attractive to animals breaking in to watch foxes eat rats.

Will there be a moment when humans realise living things have souls? Are animals not fugitives, denied their freedom? Humans no platform past misdeeds, yet devour flesh, skin animals, consume sea, earth, indifferent to those who suffered to survive. Early deaths, incurable diseases, poverty, hunger; conscription; violence, death, were the common lot, while now descendants bask in human rights which transcend nature.

In the Wild, an animal may see brilliant sunshine cutting through the trees, then at one moment sensing ecstasy, then terror.

In Bingo's Zoo, every cage, every compound, every aquarium is a prison cell in which the inhabitant is observed, fed, and medicated. Predators in the wild cut down the innocent as we cut flowers. Yet a lion, if it grows old, learns terror at the last. They are playthings of man, the tamer of lions.

I couldn't get the idea of the Chinese Communist Party out of my mind, or at least the metaphor of

Zoochosis, forced upon dissenters. Then again, I could not get out of my mind Adele, the penguin.

Snag maintains animals do not know love as humans do. I'm not so sure. Adele loved; and probably longed for freedom. Freedom preoccupied the Greeks. They fought bitterly to defend it. Now their art, their poetry are discounted because they had slaves. Wish fulfilment.

The Zoo is an ugly enterprise. At the top: Venetsianov its sponsor, Bingo its capitalist and Ulysses the rentier. The system is based on privilege; Pandas, Snakes, and Tigers, the superior caste at the top, get privileges. Of course, they are also hostages. The system is the same as when, in the nineteenth century, the French and the British brought North Africans and South Americans over and displayed them in what they called the Human Zoo.

The Sudanese say this was kidnapping and slavery. A famous pygmy was displayed in the same cage as an Orangutan. The Pygmy was called Benga and he committed suicide. Animals have limited recourse to suicide.

Annie says I show no respect and am a bully like her dad. "Not to put too fine a point on it, you are the problem," she said.

"How can that be?"

"Daddy has a school chum, a psychiatrist. They both suffered migraines in their youth."

"Really? You don't say."

"Lewis Carroll had migraines. Dr Bacon is this quack's name."

Turns out, Annie told her dad about me being chamicado. He deduces I am plying her with drugs, and passed this on to Dr Bacon.

"Are you going to make a donation to the rainforests, Dad?" Annie asked.

"You ought to see Doctor Bacon first. He has authored a book on psychosis, about the end of time, sort of thing."

"That's the first I've heard of it," said Annie.

"Bacon adduces evidence that *Alice in Wonderland* is about distortion."

"How does that help?"

"You believe all this stuff about Rainforests? When Alice drinks and gets too big, this represents the population. When Alice shrinks, this is global warming. Macropsia. Micropsia. The endless animals, caterpillars, rabbits, turtles, all humiliated. The Rabbit consults an I phone. Carroll experiments with magic mushrooms."

At this, Annie lost her temper. "Look, Dad, are you going to make a contribution or what?"

"Hear me out. Carroll was totally against Evolution. Bacon emailed me this yesterday. I quote: 'Science made this fair green earth, if not a heaven for man at least a hell for animals.' That's what Carroll said. Prescient for a Victorian, eh? Carroll was more gifted than most scientists."

Annie's dad wrote her a cheque for two thousand pounds, post-dated, on the understanding she would attend Dr Bacon, and find alternative employment.

Man's ancestors, in their caves, painted animals morphing into men; men morphing into animals.

"In our collective memory, a few fragments survive in Daedalus, and the Minotaur," Annie suggested.

"I bet Alpha males are happy with all that sex? Was Stalin into sex?"

"He was off his head."

"The communist hierarchy was a threat to his survival. His hormones rose in an extraordinary way. He survived stress with elevated glucocorticoids, which don't always go with high testosterone.

"His immune system was compromised. Instability was what he wanted. He increased stress to boost his tenure."

"Are you suggesting the communists arranged all that for him?"

"Intense social relationships help."

"Like baboons?"

"Careful!"

"You need bonding."

"Also resilience, and passion."

"In the masses?"

"Come on," I said, "let's go for a walk."

Before the woods lay a piece of ground full of greenery. In it, moths and butterflies were awakening in the warming breeze. I was in debt to Anne, who, as an Englishwoman, and somewhat scholarly at that, tutored me on these animals. Each of them was a piece of jewellery beyond the ken of outlanders such as me. And for a moment I sensed their triumph. I had met Anne on equal terms, not that we were equal. She was my intellectual superior. We met as adversaries.

As we approached, two day moths threw up their wings in surprise. The breeze enveloped us. "A White Ermine, lordly as Narcissus," said Anne; "and there, there, a Large Emerald as green as Persephone," she exclaimed.

And then, like a kaleidoscope, my imagination shook out the scented breeze. Bowing to distant royalty, the trees trembled: a ruby Tiger camouflaged in brown and cream and red fled the concourse. A Lobster in a fur coat; and a Peach Blossom instantly summering painted the shining scene. Even a red Cinnabar moth of delicious red and brown took wing between young ragworts on the margin of the woods. Such beauties stud the country in late spring under clouds of ambrosial rain.

Exhilarated, I was in the Wild. This is the spring head of beauty. We entered the cool wood. My soul flourished. This is better than Guyana, I thought. Pity there's no rainforest here.

Animal embraces spirit; spirit embraces stone, and tree. What would it be like to become a tree; to feel my cheek as rough as bark, to feel muscle, and flesh harden into wood, to feel roots where once were feet, intertwined with earth and fungi?

One day in dawn's first gleaming light, Anne proclaimed, a billion leaves will dream to curl. Ten billion seedlings will unite. What did she mean? I talk to trees. I forage. I talk to animals. I ask the green wood.

Half the UK butterflies are on the red list. The Adonis blue, the chalk hill blue, and the silver spotted skipper have joined the list of the endangered.

Shortly after this, Underform asked me to help a visitor: a Doctor Drake, who was studying coprophagy in humans and hoped to learn how we deal with it in animals. Ulysses made some introductory remarks.

"It is not uncommon," he said. "This is the Gorilla, Peter," he said, pointing to our magnificent silverback.

We stood outside Peter's enclosure for an eternity, but he did nothing to oblige. There is a place and a time, he seemed to say. Come back later. So he just sat there like a member of the MCC, deep in thought about the golden age.

"How do you deal with it in the NHS?"

"The usual. Mostly chemistry. In my time I have prescribed Haloperidol, Lorazepam, Trorazodone, Valproic acid, Mirtazaprine. Lots, lots more."

"Do they work?"

"Can't say. Humans don't present the problem too honestly. In fact, they hide it. Like mental health. Some start young, and revert. Some suffer damage to the amygdala, others have honest to goodness psychological problems: oral fixation; hyper-sexuality; schizophrenia. And you?"

"It doesn't worry us. Boredom in animals. Depression. OCD. There's a whole range of mental health problems which are surprisingly common: self-harm; obsessive swaying and circling, tearing their hair out, sicking up and eating down. Sometimes, it's nutritional. We feed them well, but I think it's the rats. It comes naturally. They eat vegetation, but can't digest it, so a second helping does the trick. The rats have taught half the zoo to take it up. It's fashionable. They're winking behind our backs. The rats make friends with the exhibits."

"It's natural," said Snag, who had insinuated himself into the discussion. "Terriers are forever foraging; and chew this kind of thing in a spirit of curiosity, with a thoughtful expression on their faces."

"Like a *maître de fromage*?" said the Doctor.

"The real aficionado is the fox, who subsists on worms or worse. Some find nutrition in dog poo."

"The same thing applies to humans. It's the modern way to get the last drop of nutrition out of the supply chain. We will all go for it we don't control global warming."

"But what if we run into an epidemic? Epidemics spring from dirt."

"In the old days I used to dowse patients with icy water. That slowed them down," said the Doctor. "Recently, a vibrator showed results."

Ulysses was not much taken by this. "We feed ours freeze-dried pancreas," he said. "That rebalances them. And we hire an entertainer, someone who does tricks at children's parties. He wears ladies' underwear, lots of perfume, brings a small child dressed as a baby, sings lullabies. That works. The Lions like it."

"My patients don't go for that," said Drake. "Some are ashamed. You can overstate the commonality between humans and animals."

"Well, how about Syncope?"

"Humans are complicated. Animals faint due to lapsed circulation, except giraffes and tree snakes."

"Animals faint out of fear," said Ulysses. "The majority of animals feel terror daily, hourly. The brain shuts down. The animal passes out. Hold a robin in your hand, it will pass out. Draw a chimp's blood, like it or not, it faints. Sharks faint for up to fifteen minutes a go. Millipedes faint. Snakes faint. Wasps faint. Crickets faint. Hens faint for many reasons."

"Fair enough," said the Doctor. "Humans faint for other reasons."

"Well, we haven't nailed it, either. But terror is the trigger. Survival is the benefit. Predators turned on by blood disdain anything they think is dead. The fox will walk away and leave a fainting duckling in hope of better prey, hot with pulsing blood. Insects are turned on by blood-engorged girls, not bloodless ones."

"What are the symptoms in humans?"

The question was inappropriate. The Doctor would not be drawn.

The animals had been humiliated again. Are humans animals? If so, how did they become unnatural? And then, I thought, I must up sticks. I am getting entangled in this Zoo.

I am interested in plasticity, the ability to modify form in response to the environment.

Dung beetles are a plastic species. When colder weather makes it hard to take, off they grow larger wings. Epigenetics seem to permit different development strategies in a single lifetime. Spadefoot toads are omnivorous. Fed flesh by scientists, the tadpoles grow large teeth, powerful jaws, and a different gut. They can then feed as ambitious carnivores.

By convergent evolution, a number of different amphibious fish move on land by wriggling, jumping and propelling themselves on hardened fins and tail, using pectoral and pelvic muscles.

Many ancient fish had lung-like organs. A few, such as bichir, still do. The Senegal bichir has real plasticity. It has gills, but also lungs and can breathe air, but chooses to live underwater. Taken out of water, they change. The bones in their fins and their muscles develop, enabling them to move along on land. Their lungs grow. Instead of millions of years of evolution, this animal changes with immediacy, in a single generation. Some ancient 'lunged' fish were the ancestors of tetrapods. So, in amphibious fish man may have an ancestor.

For some reason, eels are not included as amphibious, despite their ability to migrate long distances on land. In places like Elham in Kent, they are associated with streams that go dry seasonally but in which the eel is said to have burrowed into mud periodically, and survived.

Plasticity in eels is a critical component of their evolution.

The transition from breathing water to breathing air is said to be the most significant event in vertebrate evolution.

Eels came at it variously. They take oxygen through the gills. In air, about a third of the total oxygen uptake occurs via the gills. During the first hour of air exposure, oxygen removal from their swimbladder may be almost equal to the oxygen uptake from the air.

They also breathe through their skin.

During air exposure, eels keep the gill cavity inflated with air, which is slowly depleted in oxygen and renewed at intervals.

The eel has survived a hundred million years: man maybe ninety thousand. Man has overseen a catastrophic decline in many species, ninety-five percent in the case of eels.

The eel's plasticity has enabled it to survive enormous journeys imposed by a kaleidoscopic planet.

Its life cycle starts with the suicidal decision to breed. After lives often of twenty or more years, the mature eel ceases to eat and sets off on a journey of six thousand kilometres to its breeding grounds, surviving solely by absorbing nutrients from its own body until they spawn, then die. During this stage, their brains undergo transformation at the molecular level. For one thing, their eyes get bigger. They swim mainly in the deep, avoiding light, but come closer to the surface at night. Why? So they can see the moon, which provides directional cues. They share with turtles and birds the ability to discern the earth's magnetic field, which they also use to navigate.

Spawning somewhere near the Sargasso Sea leads to tiny larvae (3mm) which grow by feeding upon marine snow until they enter a second larval stage, when famously they assume the shape of a willow leaf.

Their next transformation is into the juveniles, described as glass eels; in other words, transparent. Later, fully grown, they turn yellow. Entering sexual maturity, they acquire sexual characteristics, i.e. gonads. There is no set timetable for this.

The larvae now use the same directional clues, in part derived from the earth's magnetic field, so they are able to find their parents' point of departure.

Their migrating speed is low, so they utilise the ebb and flow of tides and the deep currents of the ocean as birds use the winds to aid them. They also process olfactory cues, especially when approaching land. By smelling green odours, the volatile substances with earthy or musty odours produced by actinomycetes, algae or amino acids which seem to act as pheromones, drawing them into coastal waters and to streams in land.

Remember, glass eels at an early stage of the eel's life are neophytes. Their minds are processing multiple chemical and magnetic clues without maternal care or training, yet they must pass from the deep sea to the continental shelf, from coastal waters to brackish estuaries. Why do some never come inland? How do they compute their navigation from rheotactic assessment of water currents to the magnetic imprinting and lunar computations they inherited?

This data processing has been going on for a hundred million years. It is only now that mankind has clambered to the soaring heights of folly to consign them to near extinction.

The reason for these Odyssean journeys is simple. From the eel's ancient origins not far from modern-day Indonesia, the earth's tectonic plates have divided, moved and rearranged the surface of our planet. Between three hundred and twenty-five and one hundred and seventy-five million years ago, dry land was concentrated in one huge land mass now called Pangea. To its east lay the Tethys Ocean. One hundred and forty million years ago, Pangea split and opened the Tethys Ocean to the West. When eels went west, they soon enough were migrating further and further to their spawning grounds. Eventually, for European eels, the Sargasso Sea became the destination which presents such a test of endurance there is increasing pressure for new speciation. The distance to and from Europe inexorably grows wider annually.

This, in essence, is a story of evolution: not the invention of the new or unimaginable, but the immense effort of life clinging on to the convolutions of a mighty environment. They must complete the endless assault course which Fortune ordains. At the centre of this journey seems to be magnetic sense. Magnetic sense may come from a symbiotic relationship between multicellular life-forms and magnetotactic bacteria. So the bookends to evolution in this story are, on the one hand, a restless and utterly dominant environment, and on the other hand, little life-forms probably exploiting symbiosis based on magnetism.

To retard the eel's extinction requires an international response engaging the Japanese, whose science and commitment are world class.

Again and again, the question arises. Is humanity capable of the co-operation needed to redress their sins?

Instead of mourning the extinctions we cause, can we not preserve the good environments we inherit, wherever feasible, and so rescue Nature?

Let us re-examine the roadmap. Maybe every hundred million years or so, the planetary furniture is rearranged. On the plus side is the symbiotic magic of life: archaea, bacteria, viral DNA, Transposon, and agents that move them. What triggers the movement of DNA into establishing new forms? People are examining genomes, but apparently new lines can just appear from nowhere, or from unlikely places.

How did amphibians come into being? Can we bottle the answer? Is it really Tectonic plates and meteorites wot dunnit?

Some say when humans first left Africa, a hundred thousand years ago or more (just a lifetime to the eel), humans integrated with their relatives humans, allowing them to adapt to new and challenging environments.

Are not adaptive radiations, comprising many species and derived from a small number of earlier ones, prominent components of biodiversity? Hmmm?

Introgressive hybridisation of divergent species can lead to new morphologies, even new species, so they say.

With the onset of global warming, science shoulders an immense responsibility. Who speaks for them? How may they help life on earth survive? Science has failed consistently on extinction. There are no eels in Elham.

As for Darwin, he was a member of the zoological society and frequented London Zoo to observe his lady friend the Orangutan, but neither he nor the zoo engaged the public in the issue of extinction. Perhaps not surprising in an era when men regarded animals as bait for baiting.

We've had the best of it, those of us who enjoy animals before they go extinct. If the problem is humanity, we must seek a remedy. If extermination creates gaps for new life to fill, perhaps some kind of genetic alarm signal could be invented to rally genomes to go adventuring. But our priority is preservation of environments, not just increasingly moribund species. Pray that what is good will endure.

Somehow, these thoughts got mixed up with my feelings towards the jaguar lady who shared a burger with me in the cafeteria. I knew in her the mystery of the Wild must be encoded. I found myself frequenting the walkway next to her cage. But experienced no further interaction. She was inclined to sleep, and when awake, ignored me. Now the zoo is temporarily closed, we are cut off.

When the Zoo reopened, I noticed a change in the inventory. A bit like the planet. Less animals. Old favourites like Lemurs and the Marmoset vanished. Emissaries stealing in and out on secret missions?

I tried talking to the new arrivals, but they looked blank. I went to the girl who mixes the animals' food.

"My name is Heeb," I said. "What's your good name?"

"The boys call me Gaga."

She smells lovely. Must be the ingredients she mixes. I fancy her. So kind of her to let me in early, in time for feeding. It was six a.m.

"I am always here on the dot," she said. "Good morning. I have taken delivery of mealworms, sand eels, my bamboo, and such like."

"Your Anteater doesn't much like the mealworms."

She looked at me oddly. 'How do you know?' she seemed to say.

"So, are you on your own?" I asked.

"No, no. Sacha is sweeping up turds. And my son, who is off school, is lending me a hand."

Gaga rubbed her pink tired eyes. Then she yelled, "Timmy!"

A little lad no more than seven or eight appeared.

"Say hello, Timmy."

"Hello, Timmy," said the little lad obligingly, and blowing into his hands he made a farting noise, then ran away, cackling with glee.

"Don't mind him," said Gaga.

I don't.

"A terror? He doesn't take after you. Maybe his dad?"

"Haven't seen him in years. I'm going to sluice down the concrete floors. Want to give a hand?"

"Sure. I'm game."

So off we went, carting fresh sawdust and straw. Gaga took me quickly from enclosure to enclosure, delivering breakfast. Wherever the captives were dangerous, we kept to underground tunnels and the routines of using a walkie-talkie and the religious use of padlock and key. I made notes on which animals needed supplements and special diets. If Gaga is unable to turn out one morning, I might step up.

Gaga doesn't want to flirt with me. I imagine her as an animal in an enclosure, and I find her desirable in an unvarnished way.

She complains about work.

"I work fifty-six hours a week, and have no prospects. I have no pension, no savings, and if I get to be an old woman, it will be in dire poverty. I have a bad back."

"I'm sure something will come up," I said. "Don't you have family?"

"Not since my dad died."

"If I can do anything to help, I will."

"Diversity," said Snag, "according to Montesquieu, was why Rome fell. It is why Europe will fall. Think who has transformed the world: Darwin, Newton, Foucault, Tim Berners-Lee, Einstein. Jesus. All men, all middle-aged, save Jesus, most white."

"Made by women," said Annie.

"Matthew, Mark, Luke, John," Snag replied.

"And the gospel according to Mary," she countered acidly. "The girls who followed Jesus were belittled."

Her eyes brimmed. I ploughed on.

"If you look," I said, "I am only just male. Perhaps it's the clothes."

She went bright red. The tears miraculously dried.

I took her by the hand. "My dear one, we are committed to save Nature. I see magic in the natural world. I respect your disbelief, but magic is needed to inspirit Nature. God is Life."

"I disagree."

"You want to protect the world. So do I. Beware those who stand for disenchantment, and destruction of belief.

"More than anything, I wish to win you over, Annie. You more than anyone can make art and poetry for us. So work with me to revive Nature."

"For me," she replies, "the genome is the nearest thing to reawakening."

Yamhead is a Ghanaian, lovely, warm, and funny. A more like-minded comrade I could not want.

With him, I can speak my mind.

"As you know only too well, Yam," I said, "there's not much left to import from West Africa. Even grass cutter is endangered. What can I do?"

"We Africans are the vanguard. I am marketing insects as proteins," he replied. "Do you like locust? Their evolution includes phenotypic plasticity triggered by population density which they detect through the hairs on their hairy legs. Then the nymphs begin to march like high school marching girls. They're the best for eating. I love locust and honey. I'm a John the Baptist throwback."

"If there were locusts in the zoo, they would plod backwards and forwards in their enclosures, solitary and waiting to be forgotten," I suggested.

"But they have a 'Get Out of Zoo' card!" he exclaimed. "Something to do with serotonin. One minute they are anchorites, the next they become a crowd, shoulder to shoulder, wing to wing, hungry, angry, multiplying like... well, like locusts.

"Animals have a relationship with my clan back home. We're on first-name terms with locusts." He laughed.

"I know. No waterway can be polluted, no forest deforested," I replied. "You people take totem seriously. We need you. From what I understand, the Democratic Republic of Congo is the last great mystery on earth. As big as Western Europe, connected by water, roadless but hiding long-lost cities in the forest."

"Don't be silly. But there are mysteries which the West ignores. Let your legacy be the trees and the animals you save. Let forests be cleansed and become cauldrons for your magic."

I told him Annie has been investigating the dark web where people kill and eat rare animals, alive. It seems to mirror depraved sex. As if some virus leaped boundaries.

What fascinates me is the way they push back nature. All right, curiosity draws people to Francis Bacon. I am more cautious. Some artists use violence and depravity in the hope of making these things normative and inclusive of themselves. It's omophagia next.

In China, there are still people eating animals alive: snakes, piglets, and worst of all, anchored in an exoskeleton, the brains of monkeys which they spoon in as the animal shrieks. There is a dish of live mice that squeal inside the mouth. They say the aficionados are nice people. But a lovely person like Annie is disgusted by omophagia and pornography, while apparently others can't get enough.

"Search me," said Yamhead.

Circe, listening in, tried to rationalise. "Our differences with China are cultural. If evolution is competition, then compete. Action is critical. Genes leave culture open."

"Action and learning make culture good or bad," said Yamhead.

"Animals have no culture."

"We must protect them."

"The Chinese Communist Party has lifted half a billion people out of dire poverty," Annie replied. "They helped the poor more than any religion ever did. They will do the same for animals in good time."

"Hats off to the CCP. Huzza," I said.

"Huzza?" Snag replied. "Don't they hate a free press, though?"

Circe stood up. "Evil is unleashed on the instruction of one man elected by one all-powerful party. That man pretends he is the demiurge. Legion upon legion submit to him. Imitation becomes the rule."

"Cultivate the Chinese by all means," I replied, "but only if the CCP devise ways to condemn tyranny, dispel Zoochosis, by which I mean loss of freedom, and adopt compassion. They could start by promoting an Own Label Christianity."

This provoked Annie. Now there was no stopping her. Like a school mistress, she lectured me. "Equality comes through Collective Leadership," she announced. "Full powers in China are vested in the people's congresses. Centralised administration is guaranteed at every level. This is completely missing in the West."

"The West has the trump card of unfettered disagreement," I said.

"Come off it," Snag interrupted. "One unscheduled war and carbon promises go up in smoke. The indecisive short-term bickering West is doomed."

"In China," argued the Major, "they are back-pedalling on Carbon. Why are they building Coal-powered plants? Why so many high-rise builds, knocked down again?"

"I don't agree all their policies, but the planet survives if humans change. I don't like repression any more than you do, but if we don't change, the only way is China."

"So change through coercion? That means liquidating opposition."

"What's the alternative?"

"Is communism what you prefer?"

"The battle for the soul of Nature," I replied, "has begun. We have to stitch pity, compassion, even Christianity into Chinese culture.

"Morality is explicit in their policy. But not in democracy, except perhaps Brazil. And look at them."

"They are nationalists," spat Snag.

"The USA has no ideology save democracy. Their constitution politicises the Supreme Court. So they gerrymander justice. They gerrymander race. They gerrymander the Presidency. That's disgusting. Blacks are not born equal to whites in America, even today, despite their constitution."

"But they celebrate great foreigners."

"You mean Von Braun and Merkel? And Dr Porsche, the sponsor of the Elephant, the Tiger, and the Panther?"

Everyone looked pissed off.

I took Snag to one side.

"I'm not suggesting violence," I whispered. "But the chemical companies are accumulating 'forever' chemicals in the earth. We saw off tobacco. More to do."

"Do the Chemical boys?" Snag responded cheerfully. "See what you can come up with."

Little Timmy was making a nuisance of himself. He ran up to me, making his farting noises. "That Annie is a bit of all right," he said.

"You aren't allowed to run around insulting grown-ups."

"Keep your hair on."

"Your Mum is trying to protect the animals from hooligans like you."

"Who broke in the other night?"

"Yes."

"I rescued a lizard. I'm caring for it."

"Does your Mum know?"

"What of it?" And he sauntered away, hands in his pockets like an elf.

And I fell to thinking about Eleniya, imprisoned by the Amur Tiger. Kanaimas, shape-shifters, follow their enemies for years before killing them. In human form, they have lines or spots, red spots, on their skin, and are emaciated. They are mistaken for humans. I do not want to be part of a world of revenge, of invisible arrows, of torture and hate. England seems safe, but is my new love, the Jaguar, a messenger, to lead me back into the wilderness?

From the very moment we spoke, my interaction with animals has taken off. I can get through to rats, who, though dirty, are clever.

"Do you count yourself part of this Zoo?" I asked one.

"We are outsiders, poor and hungry. The Zoo is riddled with anti-rattism. All the big decisions are made behind bars. But we see the future."

"What do you see?" I asked.

"A world redesigned by Revolution."

"Freedom?" I asked.

"Symmetry. Not freedom. This prejudice has to stop. Contempt shortens lives."

The rats, unloved, are on the outside, under suspicion. They don't 'belong'. If we support them, we destabilise the zoo and drive the proper inmates mad.

Yamhead supplied me with a Ghanaian snack. Very chewy. Odd flavour. Nice. Its effects include bright lights: a shooting star. It helped me interview the Jaguar, that lovely creature.

No two cages in the Zoo are the same. Each creature has a peculiar misery; a hope crushed, a desire bottled up; unfathomable neuroses; no escape.

"In the Wild, mortality is higher," I said.

"And life shorter. But I want to roam forests where mysterious cities lie hidden, and magic awaits discovery."

"Did you never hear of Thoth, and Hermes Trismegistus?" asked Annie. "Records from the mists of history tell how Nature can be revived, and the curse of Eden lifted."

Putting her hand on my leg, she whispered, "You and I are on the same page. That's why I wrote the poem. What do you really think of it?"

"I feel a tremor of love," I said, "and its power is growing."

"Really?" She kissed me.

"I knew we were on the same page," she said.

"We are now," I replied. I began to fall in love all over again.

I was invited to meet a man who has the ear of US Presidents.

We met in an apartment at the Grosvenor House. Called Schwarzweiss, he introduced me to Katya, his wife.

"You are both so young."

"You mean inexperienced? The reason I wanted to meet is your project to save the Rainforests. I am working with Russia. I believe you know Orlik?"

"Oh, Gowler?"

"We are part of a cartel of consultancies who make things happen. Most things that happen have our imprimatur."

"Imprimatur?"

"It means authorisation, doesn't it, sweetie? Katya is a Catholic. Katya is preparing me for the Presidency."

Katya is now standing at the door, watching the elevator.

"I've never understood the Presidency. How does it work?"

"Political capital. As in capitalism generally, ownership is everything. Katya is our mother. Forgive me, I get emotional about this. Every Davos, we let a new bunch off the bit to see how they run.

"We give them the same head start. We teach them to set an agenda, how to establish their imprimatur.

"Now tell me. I heard about you from Gowler," he said. "We are working to make Russia great again."

"So Russia is back in the fold?"

"No-one to test their nuclear resolve."

"Things can't go on like this."

"China will intercede. Meantime, we are making Russia innovative. Innovation is commodified in the West. Everyone is innovative. Few profitably. Us big consultancies control innovation and do not complicate it. For Gowler, we have designed what we call the Chastity Belt. This enables him to grow an entirely new Rainforest; innovation, top down, bearing down on it, giving him absolute control. Uninvited innovation is flushed straight down the toilet. The best innovation is disruption, so we are disrupting trade across the Arctic. The West is fast asleep. We've positioned Russia as gatekeeper. Scientifically formidable, their funding dried up. So we manoeuvre them into the middle of the action, in shipping."

"Sort of marketing?"

"Oh, no. That is what companies do. Not at all. It's an art. Start somewhere unexpected. Then crunch every square mml of data our youngsters collect, and roll it out like steel into a seamless shining narrative. Then finish with a denouement which astonishes. We are working on things that could be made of rainforest. See? That's consultancy. A young person's game."

"Tell me," I said. "The destruction of the rainforest. Is it inevitable?"

"No. The North East passage is the coming thing. Will make Russia the greatest maritime power on the planet. And there are other things climate will magic up. When we see something happening, we make it happen. Russia is the go-to partner. China, India, and the EU are suitors, notwithstanding appearances. The Severoput is key. The ice will melt. Same with the Rainforests. They will be destroyed. But contrary to what the snowflakes say, all will be well. Russia understands scale. Their tank production was magnificent in the Second War. Focusing on scale, and free of ideology, they are flying.

"Russia is Europe's long-term partner. Behind the scenes, the EU is prepared for this. The current war is an unfortunate exception.

"When our President compared Britain to Israel, you know a chapter has just closed. Presidents playing to the ethnic gallery with cheap jibes," Shwartzweiss ploughed on

"America Russia and the EU know the UK is going to break up. They can't exactly make it happen, but with our help it will happen."

He turned on his charming smile.

"What will replace the Rainforest?" he asked.

"It would have to be a zoo."

"A zoo? You surprise me. Why?"

"Biodiversity will have crashed."

"We will invent new forests," he said. "Extinct animals can be reactivated. New life-forms invented. This is the age of androgens."

"I wish. You are aware that America is built upon the bones of Nature?"

"New life will be a source," he said firmly, "of medicines, and nutrition."

"Can you set Nature free?"

"I don't understand you."

"So God can come back to earth."

"You disappoint me," he said. "I had understood from Gowler you were more grounded. I am disappointed in you," he insisted. "As a consultancy, we disrupt the present and reinvent the future. We are reinventing insurance. The best brains in the world are planning a single global behemoth of an insurance company. We know nothing about insurance, but with our processes we collect data no-one knew existed, and – it is no secret – now will take a piece of the action. But, hey, must keep in touch. Good to have met."

This was fishy. I called his wife.

"I was enthralled by your husband. But he can't stand for President when he is hand-in-glove with the Russians. Can he?"

"Oh, America has always been involved in Russia. First the Whites, then the Reds. After centuries of Anglo-American understanding, the Kennedys changed our orientation. They broke into the most exclusive clubs. Then Bobby colluded with the Kremlin."

"*Déjà vu?*"

"You British think you change things. You don't. Americans engineer change. We foster morphogenesis.

"We weave a new cloth upon the loom of womanhood. A thousand strands, economic, educational, psychological, sexual. Our women have emerged, renewed. You Brits measure progress against days long gone, when your women were domestics. For you, liberation is about sex and statistics. That thinking is hopeless. We create new icons of power for a different era and a different woman. We give women freedom, speed, self-reliance and the products to make it so. You end up copying Americans.

"It's as plain as the nose on your face. Look at the speed of change at Tesla. Your motor industry died ages ago. You failed to manage labour. Capitalism was not allowed to work. Owners were mistrusted. Even the Italians outdid you. Don't worry about my husband. Every little shift and tremor of post-modernism improves the American way of life. What appear to you to be fads and wokeness are a vast new life-form, a new creature of gigantic stature. Microbes shift and grow, creating and expropriating power on an enormous scale. We redesign the world, based on capital, science, and the metamorphosis of women."

To me, her words seemed empty. I want real revolution, not fake. Britain, she seemed to say, is trapped in the imperial past. But what of her Consultancy?

I called on Gaga and asked her out. We had a lovely time. She smells of all those foods she mixes. Afterwards, a baboon remarked that Gaga was sexy. Must be those red trousers. Then I recalled the old adage a Hebu's arse is hot as fire. I felt ashamed, though not sure why. The truth is, my encounter with the Jaguar attests a new beginning. I am on the cusp of understanding the secrets of animals. I asked where the Jaguar was. She has been sold, they said. I was so disappointed.

Then Peter, the ageing gorilla, shook me out of it. Bingo had pulled off a successful swap. He traded Peter and an elephant called Ted, whose life expectancy is zero, for two elephant seals: one male, one female. The female was crushed en route by the male. The counter party insisted on returning Peter.

We showed up to welcome him back. Ulysses said this would boost his self-esteem. Drugged for his flight from the US (tolerable), he was revealed lying on a huge blanket fast asleep. We talked amongst ourselves for what must have been half an hour, but quietly.

When the time came, Ulysses let himself into the compound. Peter sat up, stretched and picked his teeth. He looked up and spotted Ulysses about a hundred foot away.

He leaped up, sobbing audibly. I can only describe what I heard as a sob. He ran to Ulysses and smothered him with an embrace and made a whining noise. He gave every impression of being deeply moved and overjoyed.

I felt he was a sentient being who longed to be reunited with his keeper. Love is commonplace in animals. What is distressing is that in South East Asia and parts of Africa there is a booming trade in primates. In reality, there are only a few thousand animals in each species, and falling numbers have made the gene pool more limited, perhaps fatally. No amount of publicity can stop this.

Chapter Twelve

I took my group to explore a tiny old oak forest in Wales. We found mud, lichens, liverworts, spongy wet moss and a glutinous algae that clings to things like jelly. Among the rocks there was pink ragged robin, purple cornflower, maroon and yellow water flowers, wild carrot, yellow kingcup.

The moss emerald and the silver blue have an electric effect.

Back home, the soil in the uplands is so poor the plants eat insects. The problem is how to protect soil, plants, fungus, animals. "The problem is us," said Snag. "No more, no less."

"You're right."

Snow White has become a wasting asset. Captivity is wreaking havoc on her. Gaga is giving her a soft diet. The musculature in her face has been affected. Without things to bite and gnaw, like a walrus, or a seal, her skull will get narrower.

"Living in a constricted pen leads to stereotypies," says Annie. "That is to say obsessive self-grooming, licking and rubbing. See how the sore places are visible, red in places, where skin is broken, black where white hair once was."

She tramps up and down. Ulysses says she is on his fifty-fifty list; that is to say, she will spend fifty percent of her time pacing repetitively. On top of that, she has dermatitis. They have discovered a crack in her left foreleg. There was good news, though. Unlike the elephant, her life expectancy is better than in the Wild. And Gaga cares for her.

The downside is she looks less like a Polar Bear. And deep down, her instinct to breed is stirring. She is the most noble of females, a Goddess. But to procreate she depends on Ulysses.

Timmy took a particular interest in her. Like a PoW in a war film, he counts the exact number of paces she takes in her miserable routines. He measures where she goes and when and how often. And he says she has a bad leg. He plans to make a fool of her.

He has researched the architecture of her enclosure. He beards Ulysses.

"You know Snow White's pen?"

"Yes."

"What is the point of that trench?"

"The Moat? It keeps the bear back."

"Why? Could she climb it?"

"I doubt it. Why?"

"The Moat would stop her, wouldn't it? Does it ever have water?"

"No. If Snow White fell back into it, she'd break her back. It's got an overhang, Timmy. She couldn't get over the lip. She'd fall."

"She's that stupid?"

Timmy was satisfied. The bear looking up would see the concrete over her head.

Timmy boasted to his mother.

"You know that Polar Bear?"

"Yes, Timmy."

"She's hurt a leg."

"No, she hasn't, Timmy."

"Yes, she has."

Timmy came to see me.

"Did you know Snow White has a bad leg?"

"No, she hasn't."

"She has. How fast can she go?"

"Faster than me."

"I bet I could beat her with her leg."

"We'll never know. Annie says her grandad is Frankenstein."

"The monster made out of dead men? A nail stuck in its neck," he says cheerfully.

The following Monday, Circe got back at long last from the Rainforest. Everyone fussed over her.

She made an effort to take photos. Her slide show looks professional. Her commentary is sly.

"Guyana was disappointing," she said.

Then she put up a slide of Maria.

"Our leader's fiancée," she said.

"Not true, not true," I protested.

"My poor tribe," she explained, "has no toilet, no shop, no running water except a muddy river."

She then showed a slide of my adoptive mentor, the Accouri.

"Oh," said Annie, "a rat!"

"Much bigger than a rat," said Circe. "It was in my hut. I was angry, I can tell you. I made my tribe remove it."

Then a slide of people I didn't know. They were not wearing clothes.

"Here are my Forest Tribe. A nightmare. This man" – she pointed to a terrified individual – "was killed while I was there. Those in power say the same thing: the natives are surplus to requirements; must be moved on and taught their place. I wanted to leave as soon as I got there.

"But look at these gorgeous trees. This is the glory of the rainforests.

"This is a rubber tree; you can see the rubber oozing out. That's over a hundred foot tall.

"This is kapok, more beautiful and bigger than an elm. You go here for your coffin and your canoe.

"And this small man is a cacao, a wide-branched tree; evergreen, glossy. Its oblong, drooping, bright green leaves. The cacao is the food of the gods, the cocoa bean.

"Flowers, foul smelling, are abundant twice a year, with flowers which can be white, rosy pink, yellow or bright red, surrounded by swarms of midges. A mature tree grows seventy elongated pods per annum, which are bright yellow to deep purple. Everything is so colourful and beautiful. They are grown in tiny farms in the rainforest as a form of agroforestry, amongst banana, palm, and rubber, to provide shade and wind protection for young trees.

"Its predator is a fungus that gives black pod rot if temperature gets too low and there's excessive humidity. Mealy bugs, thrips, scale insects are its enemies.

"This is an acas palm oleracea. Its feet like damp if not wet. Tiny little boys shin up it to bring down the blue-black fruit. It's too magical.

"So beautiful, we cannot lose them."

I summarised once more. "To save the rainforests, we need revolution."

"There's not enough Indians for that," Snag objected.

"Revolution is not started by the oppressed. Start with thinkers. Us."

"The rainforest is for animals. The revolution is for them," said Circe.

"Against whom?"

"Chief execs of mining companies, land-grabbing property magnates, wannabe farmers, loggers," replied Circe. "But if any of them found themselves in one of the thousands of wildfires, the orange blistering nightmares they deliberately set alight, in which two million animals are slaughtered annually, they would shit their sorry selves."

"Yeah. But two billion animals are killed annually round the world just for leather. Still, we have to start somewhere."

"We need a new process which starts from an entirely new place."

"What's the mission for Guyana?"

"Making it a no-human zone."

She put Maria's photo up again.

"This is Maria, our great leader's fiancée, named after the Virgin; poor child. She has no education, no mental health, disease, liquor problems, you name it. She is a refugee. She needs food, empathy, care, medicine, identity, nationality, LOVE. We can't abandon her."

"Love is not at the heart of modern civilisation," I said. "I have difficulty finding it myself."

Then I socked it to them.

"My message is this. We are looking at the collapse of the Amazonian Rainforest. Global GDP will tank: worst case minus twenty percent. The poor will die first. That is the American way.

"But let's be constructive. Let's turn our rainforest – into paradise. And get the Indians to do it. For ten thousand years they cultivated squash and manioc in the forests, growing Brazil nut, Nutmeg, Palm, in harmony with it. Revolution built on solidarity. Rainforests made a paradise by tending its trees, and gardening in the wild."

Everyone agreed, except Snag.

"Man eats his mother's breast," he snarled. "Deforestation creates capital, consumes the future. The world is mutating into a big Brazil: greedy, cruel, shrinking rainforests, shrinking icecaps, degraded land. I don't buy this idea of paradise under Indian control."

"The land is for everybody," shouted Circe. "That's revolution."

"What would you do, Snag?"

"Start from your premise. Re-arm the wild. Symbiosis. Less humans."

"Any such attempt would lead to war."

For once, Annie made sense. Find a great power who knows what they are about, she says. "Over forty years, China increased productivity and capital formation," she announced. "They are decisive, intelligent, realistic."

"But have different beliefs," I said. "We have a choice. America or China. Which?"

"Three great men in the modern world, none of them American. Deng, India's Manmohan Singh, and Tolstoy. None of them democratic."

"Which one do you like best?"

"Deng made China competitive, and corrupt, and he shot protestors. Despite India's corruption, Singh was incorruptible."

"I vote Tolstoy," I replied.

"All great men," said Annie.

I always knew Annie would vote Deng. "Singh was a good man and a socialist," she said, "but Deng transformed China by harnessing twin horses: Chinese Communist Party and Capital. He made China a greedy cherry picker."

"None of them would last five minutes in Brazil," shouted Snag.

"You cannot compare Deng with Singh," cried the Major tearfully. "Indians are democrats and democracy holds tyrants to account."

"That is yet to be proven."

"But Democracy liberated women."

"Communism liberated women first. The American Constitution left women out."

"Freedom of speech is American."

"Freedom of speech predates Milton and Locke. It is a matter of law, not the American Constitution; witness Republicans McCarthy and Trump. When the law itself is politicised, freedom loses meaning."

"India is democratic and free."

"Says you," Snag retorted. "India tried sterilisation; repressed the rights of the rural poor, promoted racism and Islamophobia, are world leaders in corruption alongside Brazil, and for years fended off foreign investment. Yet because they're 'democratic', you think they'll live up to carbon promises? Get real. Democracy protects Western interests. Go for centralism. Mandate politics which serve the people's long-term interests. If autocrats get too powerful, take them out."

"Poor Maria," said Circe. "Her father is going to be terrorised for objecting to that dam, I know he is. He can't keep his bloody mouth shut. He is a gunner for sure."

"Let me put a word in here," I said. "If we want to make rainforests paradise, then include fungus. They compete and add value by symbiosis with plants, trees, insects, animals. Von Humboldt said they form an interconnected, spiritual whole. The alien that kills Nature is man.

"The sooner we dispose of Darwin, the safer we will be. Darwin must be no-platformed, or exorcised," I insisted. "Revolution is the only way."

"Let's start with Fungi."

"Well, here is a list of fungal occupations," Annie interjected. "They include sex workers, traffickers, parasites, spies, terrorists, poisoners, electricians, biological warfare experts, hypnotists."

"Thank you, Annie. Maybe..."

"The living roots of the forests are curated by fungi. They share water, nutrients, and chemicals on which the rest depend. The ecology is a vast interlocking system.

"Do not write off the natives. When Darwin visited Terra del Fuego, he called them savages and cannibals. He packaged them as inferior. These people, naked, shoeless, fighting for survival in the bitter winter, ate their grandparents before their dogs, in order to survive. So Darwin believed. This is the vision which informs his meta verse. The triumphant ignorance of the West is his legacy. Democracy, reset by a materialist electorate, igniting forests, pouring volatile science on the flames, crooning about love, and giving pop stars knighthoods.

"It is no good arguing *ad absurdum* that atomic and genetic components explain life. Intricate symbiosis is a condition of cells, microbiota, genomes, species, ecologies, the planet. Unless, of course, your hypothesis is that man evolved to his current state by lighting promethean bonfires, and incinerating everyone else.

"It is below ground and above ground; the forest is the future. A Catastrophe is on the horizon. The world is evolving into nothing.

"Forests capture a quarter of global emissions. The fungus is carbon. One example is doing the rounds. A fungus called Dr Mengele pumps hallucinogens into cicadas which, ghoulies dropping off, become hyper-sexual, as their fungal master forces them to spread infection. How? He visits and momentarily lights the victims' brains.

"Let's watch. The cunning fungus leaves the corpses of infected ants out in the open, close to the nest, but outside its zone of immunity. Along come working ants on the way home to tea. Stumbling on the corpses, they get excited, then infected. Each new infected 'corpse' turns into a zombie which becomes forty percent fungus, and is kept alive, sort of, and like Mario is made to climb into the canopy, to an exactly prescribed height, where it obediently bites a leaf and hangs there by its teeth, while releasing spores from its body to infect more ants below.

"This fungus is predator, ingenious in predation. We struggle to match its ruthlessness. Yet Von Humboldt's holism is the greater truth."

Days passed.

We were in shock.

Circe had blown us away.

We gathered.

"Look," I said. "I want to draw a line. How does life work in reality? What's happening?

"Land-based animals change into submarine monsters. Large dinosaurs shrink to a quarter of their size and take to the air. Evolution? Devolution? Involution? Pervolution?

"Next question. Are these decisions useful? Are they decisions? How are they taken? Is there formative causation?

"A bee flies in and excites his fellows. 'This is where you go for pollen,' he says. 'No,' says another. 'This way!' Bee confronts bee. Some ram others, and prevail. Defeated bees fall out of the equation. The ayes have it. Everyone goes with the majority. Remind you of anything?"

"Humans," says Circe. "Maybe animals are human."

"Might as well say the same about my brain," says Snag. "Neurons fire neurons."

"How do starlings decide which way to go?" I asked. "On the wing, each does exactly what his six closest neighbours are doing, without hitting anyone. Simple. Murmuration survives.

"Why do insects and birds work collectively? For one thing, groups are more intelligent than individuals. Also,

Mosquitoes swarm for sex. Dragonflies swarm to eat them. Swallows swarm to eat both.

"To start egg production, female mosquitoes feed on blood. Males are attracted to females engorged with blood. Female mosquitoes are attracted to humans who have lots of bacteria on their skin, and are heavy breathers, like many human males. These engorged females enter a swarm of males, who dance in flight to attract a mate. The female carefully selects a partner and they fly away together from the swarm, copulating. Survival depends on major investment by the female. Statistically, each sexual coupling, so carefully executed, has to be compared to the population at large, i.e. a hundred and ten trillion mosquitoes, so each coupling is inconsequential, yet complex, intense. Human sex at two people in nine billion humans is also diddly-squat.

"Swarms happen on terra firma: mice, voles, lemmings, to name a few. These regularly overbreed. Often in top form physically, the population explodes. Climate and food are factors. There follows a terrible reckoning. Perhaps the whole species is harrowed. What is left is a rump of substandard individuals who take years to recover. There is no evidence that these fluctuations make future generations more survivable. Natural selection is disinterested. It suits man, who believes if there is killing, kill at scale. There is another species that doesn't fit the Darwin trope. Butterflies. Our large blue butterfly persuaded ants to feed and protect their pupae, perhaps even feeding them their ant babies. Take the swallowtail.

Beautiful. I read somewhere that in the USA its predators include the red-winged blackbird, the Pennsylvania firefly, the five-lined skink, the green darner, the goldenrod spider, the Chinese mantis, the fiery searcher, and the striped skunk. They obviously make good evo fodder. The ladies have three different outfits: the first one mimics a healthy male, a second mimics an elderly male. Males square up to females dressed as males, but on finding they are really females, get friendly. Then females dress up as old men so as to avoid harassment, unwanted advances and predation. Some females dress in black (melanic) when the gene which controls dopamine levels kicks in melanism. This leads predators to think they may taste bad.

"As for sex, Parnassines produce a glue which they apply to females' genitals to stop other males getting in. This is called evolution.

"As for human sex, men not infrequently try to 'own' females.

"The animal world has many other ploys which an amateur like me cannot understand, including symbiosis. Do you know that birds can flock inter-species? A tit, a woodpecker, and a nuthatch can fly together as a squadron. In case of danger, the tit gives the alarm. They copy feeding techniques from each other. No mutation as such, but enhanced survival based on co-operation. Symbiosis.

"Hedgehogs are in decline, perhaps because their tradition of curling in a ball has been put to the sword by motor cars. In practice, they survived without much evolution for thirty-five million years before cars came along. Up to then, curling in a ball and hibernation sufficed. Then all change. Running away became best practice. Which is it, mutation or behaviour?

"Hibernation, like sleep, requires two quite different strategies. Two different environments, night and day, each requiring different solutions in parallel.

"I don't like the word evolution, but imagine a landscape with niches everywhere, like potholes. A creature chooses a niche for its food supply, and chooses to stay there. But this niche has a peculiarity. Like a Venus Fly Trap, it closes the chooser in. Instead of killing the poor creature, it imposes a future curfew on them, and their descendants. At some distant point in the past, a starving Panda ate more bamboo than its digestive system warranted. A Panda chose to adapt permanently to bamboo, and got trapped and has to eat it incessantly and in huge quantities every day. Anteaters are trapped by ants. Polar bears by seals. Whales by the sea. Moles by the earth. Snakes by their abdominal muscles. This so-called evolution is determined not by extinction, but environment. They choose a niche, get lazy, and get stuck. Then the environment evolves.

"A landscape with invaginations that entrap. A landscape scarred by hunger, and by famine. These are the protocols of evolution. By choice, Lions are trapped in semen which they must unload at their competitors' expense. Spectacled Bears roam vast distances memorising, like squirrels, where the good food is hiding. Darwin spotted embryonic moles have eyes, snakes have pelvic rudiments, the embryos of baleen whales have teeth. So, presciently, he linked embryology to evolution. In other words, epigenetics hold some secrets from past success. But not as much as the environment. Darwin skated over this. Humans, as always, see themselves as fascinating, and more so than landscapes, which are the source of evolution.

"Yet memories recapitulate, and may be used again."

"Some human stories are symbiotic. Human males being men-dacious and ineffective at co-operation, like Nationalism as a niche. Nationalists box themselves in. Is this evolution? In the West, the Greeks, the Celts, and latecomers Germany had problems with Nationalism. The Italian Caesar massacred Celts. Caesar is a sort of gene, with long-term consequences. So, too, is Horatio Nelson, Duke of Bronte, the perfect icon of a gene. In Britain, different ethnic groups found ways to coalesce. Islam created collectives. Do these metaphors throw light on evolution?"

"Humans are truly animals?" said Circe. "If you agree, this is a step forward. Is their obsession with internecine war related to this? Are they trapped on a conveyor belt of expansion and destruction? Until we study embryos and embryonic models more extensively, our ability to understand evolution may remain stuck, I venture. Convergence (the fact that in marsupials evolution has produced creatures very similar to fully placental mammals) requires deep thought. Similarly, the fact that very different organisms use the same genetic material as each other, but quite differently, and unrelatedly, also needs explanation. And, finally, the extraordinary richness, diversity, and disparity of life in the Cambrian period indicates there may have been more than Darwin afoot.

"I didn't see a scientist the whole time I was there," said Circe. "I did see a priest."

"I administer the last rites. Fungi sequester or use between half and three-quarters of the carbon found in the forest floor. They umpire, they pick the team, they sponsor trees that grow better with a fungus partner. Not just trees, but plants more generally. More than ninety percent of higher plants have fungi associated with their roots. In rainforests, the soil is so full of fungi they connect trees together like a telephone relaying food and messages."

"So they control the forests?"

"No. They partner it. But man wants no partner.

"Fungus partnering provides a vital carbon sink. Your herbicides, pesticides, fungicides, your fertilisers, all undo symbiosis, and nature. Are scientists insane?"

I caught Circe handing round photographs showing me in a Tahitian shirt.

"Nice one," said Snag.

"That's not me. It's my twin, isn't it? How did he get involved?"

"He came to me with some cock and bull story. Said he was going to fly the Agouti out to you."

That evening, something awful happened. Peter died.

It was a heart attack.

The Zoo was silent save for the wailing of monkeys.

Things might have returned to normal, except for something odd. Gaga contacted a friend of hers at Art School. Between them they took a wax mask of Peter's face, as a *memento mori*. A papier-mâché mask was fashioned, painted, and passed to certain animals. The Zoo took on a surreal air.

I went to Ulysses.

"Are you going to tell us what's going on?"

Ulysses seemed confused. He said, "We must wait for due process."

Gaga put her arms round me.

"I can't bear it," she sobbed. "It is making me ill."

"You'll be fine."

"We surrender to the worst in us. We slide. I think it vile."

"We know how the Chinese treat animals. Why deny it?" Circe was demanding aggressively.

"They do rather well," Annie replied. "If we are to save the planet, we must learn coercion."

"So no more human rights?"

"Well," I interjected, "unlawful killings; state executions; forced renditions; disappearances; torture; restrictions on peaceful assembly, on religious freedom; unfair elections; trafficking in persons; violence against women, criminalisation of sexual activity; and prohibition of trade unions. Human Rights are a political afterthought in the West and don't apply elsewhere."

"In China?"

"No, in Saudi, an American ally of sorts."

"You make my point," said Annie.

"So how do the Chinese reach out to Nature?" asked Snag. "When they're not eating animals alive, that is?"

"We eat oysters alive."

"When shrimps, fish, snakes move inside the mouth, they are fresh. The Chinese look at Nature in a different way."

"That's propaganda!" cried Annie.

"Shamans," Circe said, "are the Forests' last defence. They should be run as Heritage Sites as a reparation for colonial misdeeds. But there are legal traps. Legal control in Russia? Indonesia? Brazil? Do they have that much in common?"

Chapter Thirteen

Annie knocked on her father's study door.

"I need advice."

Her father's brows beetled in surprise. "I didn't think I knew anything worth knowing," he sniffed.

"UNESCO World Heritage Sites. Are they lawful?"

He began to fuss about the room, straightening furniture, tidying away magazines and books. Then stood still and picked at his nose.

"Law is a muddle," he said. "The European Court of Justice is politicised. The ECJ equivocates when it comes to treaties between governments. Bureaucrats despise politicians.

"They outlaw criticism. Connolly found that out. November, 2011: The ECJ ruled that the Commission could restrict dissent in order to punish individuals who 'damaged the institution's reputation'."

"So justice is for the lawyers?"

"It did no end of good for his book, which sold at $400 for a secondhand copy in America until reprint. But ask what they think in China, India, Indonesia, Brazil."

"What will they say?"

"Less than America." He looked disgruntled. "The Yanks say the autonomous individual is now master of lawyers and politicians alike. That's where to start."

"That is absurd."

"I agree. It contradicts religion."

"Good."

"It contradicts Socialism, Marxism, even your atheism. Face facts. The law's an ass. They start with a Constitution cobbled together for the purposes of National expediency. Then half of them are tied to some outdated precepts till Kingdom come."

"But aren't there academics who hark after Natural Justice?"

"They are just academics. Expediency and revolution made the legal system political. At that point, Natural Justice becomes your political party's idea of morality. If your party can agree on what that is.

"Morality is inconvenient. Politicians and, I dare say, the Supreme Court don't get it, for the good reason that they don't like it.

"The Supreme Court of the United States said Congress was wrong to restrict the free speech of citizens, who have a right to read and see depravity.

"Trump came along and saw to it that the balance of the Supreme Court was changed. They overturned abortion rights, basing this on the absence of abortion from the Constitution. Guns are in it, so more guns, please.

"The Americans can't face the fact that a treasonable constitution needs violent protection. So make the presidency and the Supreme Court politicised as much as you like, you just end up replacing principle with so-called demo-crazy. The result? Gerrymandering. Once the law itself is gerrymandered, there is no hope. Trump supplies the demo; the Constitution supplies the crazy.

"The USA permits depraved rubbish which harms children. They obstruct abortion to protect the unborn. Justice Anthony Kennedy said liberty is the right to define one's personal concept of existence, of the meaning of the universe, and of the mystery of human life."

"That's Hegel," said Annie.

"It's garbage, designed around sexual recreation. Time you got a proper job, Annie. I can get you one as a researcher for our Member of Parliament. As for law. it is an ever-rising ocean. Laws are glaciers that melt into the courts and drown their customers.

"One thing you must understand about the law. It is in the most profound sense evolutionary. Napoleon made a mockery of this. He set up an authoritarian state underpinned by a bureaucracy trained not for democracy but despotism. It evolved into the European Commission."

Anne made swiftly towards the door.

When she came in next day, she looked as if she'd aged years.

She is now committed to a series of consultations with Clementine, the psychiatrist, to whom she had been referred by Dr Bacon.

Clementine is, she says, a great beauty, grey-eyed and with an elegant face and lovely skin. She moves amongst the rich. "Fun-loving, charismatic, adventurous, she turns me on.

"*Alice in Wonderland* is allegorical. There may be a worldwide conspiracy against Nature, but no evidence of it. *Alice*, written for children, is nonsensical and fun. Psychiatrists discuss Lilliputian hallucinations, and the Wonderland syndrome, but that's a waste of money. Associated hypotheses include derealisation, depersonalisation, hyperschematia and somatopsychic duality, as well as illusory changes in the size, distance, or position of stationary objects in the visual field; illusory feelings of levitation; and illusory alterations in the passage of time. You can ignore all that.

"Cut to the chase. Your employer, Mr Heeb, is the culprit. I want to meet him. You suggest he is schizophrenic, with delusions including millenarianism topped with a death wish. He may well be hearing voices and a call to revolution. It is early days, but I want you to give serious thought to finding another job.

"We also face dangerous, chiliastic ideas on your father's side.

"So, between us, we have to confront violence and paranoia. Nothing new there.

"I have drawn up a reading list for you. In it you will find a fascinating and hugely enjoyable account of Bandy Xenobia; the fantasy of a modern-day schizophrenic claiming to be directly descended from Zeus, plus modern delusions bound up with comets, sexuality, famine, and the imminent collapse of civilisation.

"By immersing yourself in such ideas, we will reach mutual understanding.

"I have a number of friends in high places, the very people your employer wishes to unseat. Between you and me, their scepticism, not least about democracy, as a health hazard, is admirable. Politics is not all bad, if it is grounded in the psycho-spiritual. Then it becomes medicine on a large scale, in a way like religion as it used to be. By the way, I congratulate you on your atheism.

"Another thing. How may we draw your employer back from the brink of breakdown? His delusions can lead to depressive disorders, both in himself and those around him. Festinger's cognitive dissonance may kick in, leading to a sense of cataclysm. There have been suicides in these circumstances. Millenarianism, which draws on Shamanism and Taoism, is unwelcome. It does not surprise me he is into substances."

She then made a highly sensitive observation. "You're going to defend your employer to the last," she said, "not least because you find him attractive. You say he is a man of the world. I say the third world. Imperial psychiatrists like Tooth and Beaglehole long ago pointed to the absence of schizophrenia in those countries untouched by colonialism. The equivalents of delusions were identified as symptoms of catatonia: waxy flexibility, mitgehen, echopraxia, echolalia. Do not underestimate your employer.

"Koestler gave his account of USSR brainwashing. It is now practised on Uighars. It will not surprise me to learn Heeb has been brainwashed."

"So what I think we are mapping, dear Annie, are delusions, voices schizophrenia. I want you to tell me if there is any sign of further deterioration. Heeb may enter a crisis which mimics psychosis. I sense he is already withdrawing from reality. Let's fix some dates. As you know, your father is funding these initial consultations, so we must be extra business-like."

To my surprise, Circe laid out a complaint against the Major, who, she says, overstepped the mark.

She would not go into chapter and verse. "You know what men are like," she said. "He tricked me."

I could feel Circe's charm myself. It was in part perfume, and the sound her old-fashioned stockings made.

"Do you want me to speak to him?"

"Tell him, stay away or it's the cops."

"But he's such a nice guy."

"No," she said, "a pig. Ask Annie."

So I did.

Annie was offended by my enquiry.

"Never mind. I want you to meet Venetsianov, Annie. Shall I arrange?"

"Do," she said, with sudden warmth.

Later, I heard Circe had gone back to her husband. They broke up when he was caught in Libya. A fearless opponent of Gaddafi, he was shot supporting dissidents and hasn't fully recovered.

Circe would not divorce, yet pays for his full-time carer.

When I quizzed Sausage about this, he said Circe is a Goddess.

So he has volunteered to move in with the two of them. Why? Because he loves her. Time and again, he reveals this selflessness.

That night, the sky was crowned by an almighty storm. Riven by lightning, it foretells war.

I had learned a lot about the threat to animals and trees. How to cage humanity? I concluded it must be by Revolution.

It was about that time a change unfolded across the world. The man on the omnibus stopped laughing and began to weep as if something was seeping into his eye.

Yamhead brought me a Ghanaian python. It wrapped itself around me, tightly. Its nickname, ironically, was Things Fall Apart.

"Humans worship Gods of reason," it hissed. "The God of the Sham, the God of the Levant, and the God of Arabia. These Gods of patriarchy, and of violence, condemn coiling serpents with our attractively open mouths and forked tongues to everlasting prejudice."

"Which God do you object to?"

"The God that brands us as evil. The God that could not be arsed to include Nature in his agenda. He has the face of an old, old man."

"Did he not redeem you?"

"That's the problem," he said. "You attach swords to the trunks of elephants, forcing these noble animals to be executioners. You crucify dogs. Aristotle saw animals as inferior, inhabiting an inferior moral realm. Yet Aristotle is lionised in the West and prized in Islam.

"I feel the niche in which man has made himself impregnable is that of violence, male violence. For most of history, slavery, colonialism, imperialism, and animal sacrifice were human memes."

"Did not Aristotle say the souls of slaves are incomplete? His model of slavery is like his model of animals."

"The role of God," said the snake, "should be to cage humanity. Closing down Eden was a big mistake."

I relayed the snake's ideas to my working group. "We should get a piece in the *Church Times*," I suggested.

Annie broke in. "Samuel Palmer, the landscapist, specialised in nooks, crannies, wheat, lambs, and the heaven of the man-centred God number 301301d. (The name of God may not be uttered, so a code name must suffice.) Palmer worshipped Nature, but only when it suited as a human meme. I have studied his paintings."

"Thank you, Anne." I stroked her hand reassuringly, then wished I hadn't.

She sighed. "I don't care who knows it," she said, "but my ambition is to be your successor. I am next most qualified to save the Rainforests."

"Yes, dear," I said.

In the mixing room at the Zoo, the smell of Animal foods had proved an aphrodisiac. Not rats, which Gaga reserves for the Hyenas, but everything else, all mixed together. So I found myself drifting to the mixing room in the early morning, looking for a cuddle. I thought cuddling Gaga in the very early morning was harmless.

"What are you doing?" she asked irritably. Her sleeves were rolled up and her arms were very pink from all the work. She had a bandana in her hair; and was perspiring and smelled heavenly.

Ulysses rushed in.

"Where's Gaga?" he shouted.

"Not here."

"Timmy's in Snow White's pen. Don't panic. But Timmy is out of control."

Everyone took off to see. Ulysses was still shouting, "Where's Gaga?"

When we got to the Pen, Snow White was craning her neck to look down into the Moat. You could just see the top of Timmy's head below.

One of the keepers came towards me. He was carrying the humane killer, and what looked like a .303.

"You're not going to use that," I said.

"Try stopping me," he said.

We walked along the fence till we were level with Timmy.

"Climb up, Timmy," said the keeper. "Climb up, for God's sake. Try and scale the fence. I'll fetch the ladder. You can get down on the other side."

"Not a problem," said Timmy. "I can outrun her."

"No, you can't."

"Yes, I can."

"Get Mum. Tell her put the meat out."

At that point, Ulysses reappeared. "Gaga's putting meat out," he said.

"I don't think she's hungry," I said.

"You're right," said a keeper. "She's Hypercarnivory. Overfed."

"Go on! Try climbing up the fence," shouted Ulysses.

"No," piped Timmy. "I can outrun her."

At that, Snow White stood up, all twelve foot of her, and made a sound like a generator. She was magnificent. So high that when the pigeons flew up, they only just got above her shoulders. Brilliant white she was, save for her black muzzle and grey tongue, and, it seemed, dark eyes shining with boundless appetite. Then she flung herself forward like a diver.

When she hit the ground below, she screamed in pain. And just lay there, her chin on the ground.

Timmy started clambering up the fence. Suddenly, his bravado was gone. He seemed a small child desperate to get away.

And then Snow White, all the while groaning in pain, got up and reached up after him. With one paw, she caught

Timmy's leg and blood gushed out in a red line, an arc sunlit in the bright air.

And then there was a crack like a car driving full speed into another.

I looked round and there was a keeper putting his gun down and looking about for reassurance. "I only winged her," he said. "You saw her. It was game set and match. We can't have imperialism in zoos."

Timmy barely survived. We didn't see him for a year, and when we did, he looked a little old man. He suffered then from PTSD. Gaga stopped fraternising with Ulysses or me or anyone. She took the brunt of criticism, was interviewed several times by the police and carried with her the shame of failing Timmy.

I compared Snow White with the feral young who hunt and stab for perverted thrills.

Weeks went by. Snow White had surgery and a metal pin was put in her leg. We thought she could be sold to California, but she was damaged goods, poor thing. She began to show signs of Zoochosis; and in particular a fear of the Moat, the site of the accident. Rumour had it she was on antipsychotics and Prozac. Gaga was made to sign a non-disclosure agreement.

"That's not surprising," said Snag. "It's a lot cheaper than taking the animal off pills and having to redesign the whole enclosure at great expense."

I went to visit Snow White. She was asleep. I woke her by whistling. Intense eyes examined me.

"What?" she said.

"You look so nice asleep. Did you ever hear of the tale of Snow White? She was awoken by a kiss."

"You don't know pain. I wish I could go back on the ice. Have pity."

"Is there anything I can do to help you?" I asked. "I am sorry for you."

"Stop them experimenting on me. Ulysses is importing a Grizzly Bear, to foist on me. He wants to change our species. They plan to open up my children's skulls to make room for bigger brains.

"Get me out of here. Let me get at those who exploit me. Reward the man who saved me."

"Saved?"

"I was shot. You did not notice?"

"What man?"

"The sentry. He instructed you."

My mind went blank. Yet I knew there was an onlooker.

"Play your part and I will get you to Antarctica," I said, "along with some males. There will be no humans to bother you. It will be paradise."

"I wanted to eat your child."

One good thing came out of it. Underform lost his job. Like most men whose socks have holes in them, he is short of greatness.

I blame myself. I saw Snow White's attack as attempted murder. I failed to understand her. My idea of Revolution requires a cause, but showed no sign of combustion.

Next day, the weather turned. It took on startling hues. After weeks of pastel blue, the heavens were speeding up and writhing. Clouds of iron converged, colliding, then coinciding in dark whorls of mayhem. Winds bristled vertically and spread black carnage, dancing and threatening in the upper airs. Below, man's sharp fingers set unnatural devices to explode across the planet: vast Tornadoes, Whirlpools of howling wind, clawing Tsunamis, Atlantic-wide. These herald new endothermic highs, then icy paths to random entropy.

One clue is the force which tears off skin, pulls out eyes, flays skulls, with scouring knives of wind. Snag understands. "Humanity has reached unnatural heights," he says. "Now on parish Earth temperatures are rocketing. The afterbirth of flesh will burn off and the land, wrung out, will be incapable even of putrescence."

"Keep it in proportion," I say. "The Chinese will sort things out."

When next I saw the Major, the poor man was woebegone.

"Why so sad?" I asked. "You've got Circe. You're moving in with her and her husband, I hear. Not too bad, eh?"

"I am in love."

"Love," I said, "is fanciful. Desire trumps it. Loyalty outlasts it."

"You forget the laws of Physics."

"What? Your idea that two particles once joined will never be wholly separated? You are not a particle, Major."

A month later, on one of his walks in heavy rain, deep at night, the Major and Bite were blinded by headlights, and fell into the road. Bite was killed outright and the Major soon after. The driver said the dog pulled across his owner's path.

Snag says the weather did for them and will soon do for us all. If you watch at night, you will see meteorology piercing the fragile nimbus of our life.

By January, the long thin fingers of winter coldly plucked the alopecia of the thinning forests, swarms of hail picked at the frozen soil, cirrhosis inflamed the evening sky, muddy water stirred the lanes, and, in memory of summer, the failing earth wept its eczema of waste. Clouds of reflux yellowed with the pityriasis of desert; the dust choked English throats. These were the signs of global warming.

***

To restore good governance, my twin sent me my Accouri. It was an emotional moment. Her family and I grew up together. Like her parents, she was ginger all over and each foot had seven toes.

"I heard you need help?"

"Your mother always had my back. How touched I am you've come."

"I hear you want revolution."

"Well, I'm not so sure. Maybe war…?"

"I have things to do back in Guyana, but I will take time off to help you."

And so she did.

"Keep it secret," she advised. "Any war that starts openly, fails. Hide your intentions."

The animals discussed eating the keepers. My Accouri said, "Who would feed you then?"

"Will you lead us?" they asked.

"There is an elephant seal, who claims his granny was boiled alive for her oil. He will lead you if you choose war."

"Let Heeb ask him."

I made a date with Gaga, the Aphrodite of our Zoo. I asked her about the elephant seal. She smelled so beautiful, I made a pass at her. She looked very cross, but then responded. Shortly after this, I had sex with her. I was very happy.

On cue, my Jaguar reappeared.

"Where were you hiding?" I asked.

"I was lent to Saudi Arabia."

I was overjoyed. Then I fell asleep and, dreaming I was lost, saw animals swarming in a cooling tower, only to be crushed and pounded by a vast wrecking ball. A crowd of men rushed in with knives and metal bars and attacked us.

I told Satin about the power of love, how it solves everything. She looked confused.

"I don't know what you mean. You need protection because without an Accouri you are frightened."

"I feel there is a bond between us," I replied. "You are my countrywoman."

She kissed me. Her breath was not nice, but I was entranced.

"You make me happy," I said. "Here in England I love the skies. I am immersed in Nature's beauty.

"But now the North wind blows: the clouds are black. Terror rises out of the East, threatening the planet, and in the South breaks from its moorings in catastrophic turbulence.

"Let us defeat terror. Let a gentle breeze vanquish and separate the clouds and let an azure cyan shine at the azimuth behind them."

"Keep your feet on the ground," she growled, and then she bit me. Actually, she bit my ear. I bled copiously.

That night we talked.

"Back home, we could marry and have children right away."

"I would like that," I replied. "Will you marry me?"

She extracted promises.

I then talked with her on the subject of shape-shifting.

"It's horrible. I was born in a perfect body. None of this slippery skin, tiny teeth suitable for eating veg, thin hair, slightly rotten smell, weak eyes, weak nose, weak ears, rank feet."

"Ah! You're on a mission, are you?"

"I am a Jaguar," she said proudly.

She has assumed the mantle of a leader. Annie is disgusted. "You have taken up with this strange woman," she says.

Satin berates me. "Show humans where to get off. The obsession with cars, clothes, toiletries, phones, holidays. Animals end up as meat or trophies or shoes. Imagine your mum as shoes.

"The snake is to be appointed Senior Independent Director," she says. "If anything happens to the Professor, pow! The SID steps in."

"What Professor?"

"Oh, haven't you heard? Your Accouri got him elected. Professor Pericles. Very clever. Big man in the South."

Later, I was in the cafeteria with Annie when Satin came in. Annie is insanely jealous.

"I have some news," said Satin. And she bent down and whispered, "You are to be a father."

I was thrilled. Annie looked suspicious. So I repaired with Satin to my room, where we made love.

Then we went to meet Pericles.

He was gross. But clever. I could see Elephant Seals know about coercion. I decided to test him. "Congratulations!" I said. "We need you. Are you familiar with Kissinger?"

"I am an animal. Animalism was invented by elephants, though some say it was coined by Hannibal. It was later applied to humans who slaughter indiscriminately. It was Caesar who applied the idea to the wholesale slaughter of humans. The Romans cut their teeth on animals. I find that very satisfying."

"What? Slaughter?"

"No. The fact that genocide evolved out of slaughtering animals.

"Napoleon then taught the Prussians. And so it goes on. The animals tell me you don't like Darwin. I agree. Intelligent design is obvious to anyone except scientists. Intelligence was necessary after the Dinosaurs, who were proof evolution is the essence of nihilism and evil. And, whisper it not in Askalon, humanity is a dreadful mistake, too, also destined for extinction."

"How soon?"

"Imminently. I am forming an actuarial department of bees. All animals need to learn mathematics, also medicine and astronomy. Islam declared such activities to be theirs. Exchange of best practice was their legacy. I intend the same.

"The conquering Normans invaded Ireland and Southern Europe. North-men invested in architecture, forts, and cathedrals. They helped Ireland by introducing them to the idea of towns and roads. Ants and termites teach men a thing or two as well.

"In short, we match humans on many fronts. Their business model for thousands of years was based on invasion, fierce masculine competition, and periodic slaughter. The introduction of female suffrage, a hundred years or so ago, did not improve human behaviour. Stalin, Hitler, Mao, all reverted to norm. For some strange reason, women saw a golden opportunity to have more of what human lads have, i.e. sex and money. We desperately need them to change men fundamentally. Look at COP26. Without brute force to unite them, humans will never pull it off. China, India, Russia, not to mention Iran, Israel, Afghanistan, cannot work together."

"None of them democracies," I said.

"Demo crazies are very short-term," he replied. We need the opposite.

"Oh, dear."

"No, no," chortled the Professor, and he ate a cuttlefish. "Countries with the word 'democratic' in their title are trouble. The Senior Service once gave me the lowdown on the Tasselled Wobbegong, a carpet shark that lays out its territory on the sea floor, with wonderful camouflage. You'd never guess it is hiding under its own beach. Swimming by, you see deckchairs and sandcastles and say this is a holiday paradise. Then BAM, you are gobbled up. Humans are so deceitful. They call themselves the Democratic Republic of this or that, then lay out bejewelled attractions like votes and freedoms, and then eat anyone who buys it. This is the challenge facing the Coercive Party.

"Their Achilles' heel is pets. We will train pets to become intimate with them and infect them.

"The United States are particularly vulnerable." The Professor sucked in air through his enormous nose. "The USA's economy is based on a travelator, on which poor immigrants travel out of poverty towards the American

Dream. It relies on deliberate inequality to drive the travelator along. So it is completely obverse to Natural Justice. The Americans say inequality makes them rich. This is not true. Scale made them rich.

"Without inequality, the American system jams up. Now they are waking up to actual racism, in which black people are forced to take the knee. Having too many guns is another mistake in a constitution cobbled together to disguise cynicism as idealism. Sophocles wrote a tragedy about it. Racism, to their undying shame, will never die until they tear up that constitution, depoliticise their legal system and repent. The underclass are ripe for disillusionment.

"Now come and meet my friend Ursula, the Eagle Owl," said Satin.

We were all taken to meet Ursula.

"Are you German?" I enquired.

"Prussian," she replied. "We wiped out the original inhabitants. Hegel worshipped authority and called it the march of God on earth."

"Oh, no," I said.

"Hegel was a moderniser, and we, as a people, are very modern."

"Are you Germans not in two minds? About nature, for example?"

"We are. Once the absolute authority of the state was understood, our defining culture became militarism. Later, we chose the Kaiser, a bit of a duffer, to be chief warmonger. This was the next step in German psychopathy which started long, long ago. But we did pioneer universal suffrage!"

"Yeah, yeah," said Pericles.

"Persuaded to turn our back on militarism, we adopted a feminine approach. We appointed a woman as Chancellor, who invited in hordes of refugees, without consulting our allies, ducked expenditure on defence, cooked up selfish deals on energy, and sucked the hind tit off the Euro, which is precisely valued to sell German cars, at the expense of Southern Europe. So now we are in a secret marriage and unable to contemplate divorce. All in a democratic day's work. Germany is, I am proud to say, congenitally undemocratic, but successful."

"Are you serious?"

"Our most serious reparation is self-criticism. The Chinese are obsessed by us. Between us, we have been operating a win/win racket (cleverly presented in Europe as a morality play, about frugality).

"China and Germany are the biggest exporters of manufacture in the world. We undervalue our exchange rates by which we ruthlessly accumulate surpluses, at the expense of other Nations. We see this as the real economy while we predate on others.

"China, fascinated by us, copy us.

"Through Germany, China seeks to subordinate the EU to Chinese interests, with Germany as co-conspirator, viceroy and economic beneficiary.

Chapter Eleven

"At this point, the similarities cease.

"China's aim is to be global hegemon. Fifty years ago, Toynbee identified China as the civilisation destined to lead the world, because, unlike America, it was more focused on unification and stabilising its sphere of influence. They hope to encourage social goals across the globe in place of Western profligacy.

"To their credit, the Chinese Communist Party foregrounds morality in politics, by which I think they mean the family, in a Confucian way. China has made an extraordinary contribution to the tripling of the global economy and raising nearly a billion people out of poverty. All this while running a multinational Empire.

"Compare this with the USA.

"In America, nothing gets in the way of short-term money-making. Blacks are not born equal to whites. Socialism is effectively forbidden. Élitism and technology are weaponised. Von Braun served the SS and the V2, then NASA. Dr Porsche, sponsor of the Elephant, the Tiger, and the Panther, is lionised. Thyssen and Nazi industrialists were empowered by America to rise again.

"We Germans accept the role of Sleeping Tiger, by adjuring militarism in favour of economic hegemony supported by little France.

"Peer under the blanket and see how German trade recovered post-war. America discouraged socialism in post-war Germany, cut out nationalisation, allowed cartels, and more or less banned price controls. This unleashed economic growth built on cheap immigration from the East, of workers well trained by the ancient regime, who, swamping the labour market, kept the trade unions honest. This set Germany on the path to revival and wealth. Instead of the jackboot, Merkel adopted a new policy in the worst traditions of democracy by delaying major decisions until proven to appeal directly to voters *post hoc ergo propter hoc*."

Chapter Fourteen

The Zoo was closed next day due to fumigation. The Aviary, Bingo's pride and joy, had been designed to replicate Africa, South America and the Caucasus. There were rocky labyrinths, and streamlets flowing through little landscapes. A Stygian hole was meant to represent a deep cave in the Amazon, a hundred metres down. There is a grove of evergreens, and an area of bog and pond, shared between frogs, a small snake and some lizards. Among these landscapes, cages had been artfully constructed and unusual species displayed, including a four-eyed turtle and birds of paradise. I worried the frogs would get eaten.

Today, a crowd of avian visitors perched nearby, creating a reunion of the free and the enslaved, the latter peeking out from their temperature-controlled accommodation. In a state of excitement, the hummingbirds hummed, having spotted swifts, their distant cousins, flying acrobatically above. Like the brown bear, the hummingbirds practice hibernation, dropping their metabolic rate to one fifteenth of normal, and so are frequently pronounced dead. The swifts perform all personal functions in public, without landing. So, not much privacy there. Like larks, swifts and house martins are in precipitate decline and could be wiped out in a decade. In all of Nature there are none more beautiful nor more moving than these birds. Their sounds are an exquisite threnody. Some say they are of the line of theropods from a mere one hundred and fifty million years ago. They survive till now because they sing ancient songs at the command of God. But, ominously, they can no longer rely on his protection, since he is being gradually ostracised by the West. After marine life, they are destined to go extinct.

Who is to blame? According to Snag, it is science first and foremost, the main channel being farmers.

Farmers had a hand in it by despoiling age-old feeding habits, destroying woods, and hedges, and changing the sowing season upon which birds rely; but most of all by overusing unproven science. Savage chemical attacks upon the insect population foretell the death of birds.

In addition, insect habitats are degraded, while farming decimates the pollinators.

Some say in the dawn of time there were many gods, and these explored the earth as birds, singing and enthusing as they went. Those who have survived are in part divine.

To me, the lark is their apotheosis.

Men have conspired to reduce genetic variability in owls, puffins, doves, larks and a thousand others. The decline in genetic variability amongst smaller populations results in the impairment of ecosystems, loss of productivity, less food energy, less converted into the biomass, and more stress on human food production. So inroads are made upon my forests as mankind thrashes about to find more agricultural land to feed himself, make money, and destroy the world.

But birds are remarkable: New Zealand Keas, Ravens, Cockatoos, Parakeets, Grey Parrots, and Ursula, one of the most intelligent birds on the planet, had flown in. Rheas and Ostriches strained to participate from adjacent enclosures. Collectively, they came over as a bunch of exhibitionists, spies, explorers, and humorists. Their secrets, such as manipulating different tools for sexual gratification, are yet to be understood.

Gia, the Kea, from New Zealand, famous for opening bottles of beer with her beak, is strangely attached to me, perhaps because she knows I am not quite human. As a result of scavenging on deer and sheep, Keas have learned that the fat around the kidneys is particularly tasty. They land on the back of a grazing animal and drill through the muscles to feed on this delicacy, accidentally causing widespread septicaemia.

How did I know Gia liked me? By regurgitating on my jumper. I know a number of animals in the Zoo have psychological problems and regularly sick up. Gia had no such neurosis. Hers was a gift. Full stop. She did it out of love. Thank goodness the fashion is yet to catch on with humans.

"Hello darling," she cried, and flew over, displaying the lovely olive brown of her outfit. "Can anyone compete with this circus?" she cried.

"Hello Gia," I said joyfully. "Cleaned out any ladies' handbags recently?"

"Yes. I am now known as 'Mina the Cleaner'," she said proudly. "Come, let me introduce you." And so, turning to her airborne assembly: "Gentle birds," she said, "I am proud to introduce you to Mr Heeb, a research scientist dedicated to saving the Rainforests. He is a personal friend. Come, give him welcome," she cried. And a most wonderful chord of song rent the air.

She continued, "Gentle birds, we have spent two thousand years debating the project of Cloudcuckooland. Our numbers since 1970 declined by seven billion. No use blaming farmers. It is the gaping mouths of mindless humans that are the problem. Every late bird has fluttered into the watering mouths of men.

"New scientific evidence shows Mankind is destroying the forests and the seas, the icecaps and dry land. We can protect the air. Yes. By founding a city in the sky, we will escape the curse of Adam."

"Hooray!" they squawked. But I thought, oh no, that old canard.

"Meanwhile, raise your game," she cried. "Defend hens, ducks, geese, chicks from the monsters who imprison us in concentration camps, suck our eggs empty, scoop us up and cook us. You penguins, shearwaters, pelicans, albatrosses, and ospreys, join the cause. You gulls, confiscate their fishing catch, ingest their pets; crap on their fruit, veggies, ice creams and fish and chips. Give them hell."

At this, the skies sang and a Rook flew up and somersaulted his black arse in the air, to general applause.

He then took the rostrum; and in a stentorian voice, announced:

"Please fly by to the anthem.

"Who'll kill Robin Goodfellow?" he crooned.

"I," squeaked a sparrow, "I'll shoot up my arrow. I'll shoot Robin Goodfellow."

"Who'll catch his blood?" cried the Rook. "Say a prayer for flying Fishes, and their little dishes.

"Aaaaaaand who taught fish to fly in shoals? Do not forget Fink Nottle."

"Who do you mean?" they asked.

"I mean Fink Nottle the bluebottle."

"I'll help him die," buzzed the bluebottle, in a small but summery voice. "With my feet enterococcal, I'll help him die."

"Do not leave out the moths, drain flies, and flying microbes," crooned the Rook.

A beetle shouted faintly into the mike. "Who'll strip him bare?"

"We," sang the microbes
in close harmony.
"We'll drown him out loud. We'll fly in a crowd;
And when we get there
we'll strip him quite bare,

so no laying out robes."

"And who'll gnaw his bones?"

"We," said the worms,
"along with our germs
we'll gnaw his bones."

A devilish virus then spake.
"We'll torch his home.
We'll wreck his biome.
We'll send in believers
with the deadliest fevers. So who wants to hire us?"
spake the devilish virus.

And all the birds sang, "Weeee doooo! Whooo…ooo!
You'll not find us sobbing,
for we'll all be a gobbing
on their ten billionth grave."

And they squawked and cheered in defiance. Gia called for a vote. "We will be the eyes of all wild animals in Heebie's revolution."

I wandered off into the Aviary, only to find an apartment occupied by a family of frogs. The frogs are terrified of the Birds of Paradise, who in turn are mortified that the frogs escape them. In both apartments live a host of insects, so obsessed with avoiding edification they fail to notice the brilliant array of South American plants such as sundews, bladderworts, pitcher plants, and even a bromeliad species, all supplementing their diet by trapping and digesting distracted insects. And so the whirligig of hunger and consumption races in compliance with Darwin's pantomime.

In the distance I could hear the birds singing, and I'm ashamed to say I wept copiously. I used to view birds as mere decorations upon my trees. But our hearts are near breaking at the thought of skylarks plunging towards extinction, some of the most exquisite creatures God has given us decimated by a plague of cruelty and selfishness.

From the Avian conference, I sought out the Professor, in my determination to investigate the cause of Revolution. He did not seem persuaded.

I whispered, "Have you led a revolution before?"

"Yes, yes. All the time."

"I've just attended a conference."

"The Wild," he said, "relies on the immense unintelligible forces of Nature interacting over millions of years. Not something knocked up by a so-called scientist yesterday."

"Surely evolution is a stable system?"

"Don't mention the word evolution. We live in the age of Accidie. The unravelling of life on Earth. Until now it was the World evolved. But now, thanks to man, Life on Earth is extinguishing the planet."

"Didn't Darwin say these conditions give rise to progress?"

"He was overrated, an emotionally unintelligent racist."

"Was he, though?"

"Did you never hear of him banging on about the Irish and the Scots? Prejudices and stereotypes all mixed up, to support an ill-informed critique of overbreeding. Breeding like rabbits, he said. As a result of this kind of racism, the Irish have become the third richest nation measured by GPD per cap."

"I don't believe that."

"Their wrongful and vicious tax arrangements with America incite others to want the same back-handers. American-style capitalism suppurates across the globe, guided by nationalism not American but imported into a Society infected by imported quarrels.

"Talking of breeding like rabbits, contrary to Darwin, Neanderthals had big brains, wonderful physiques, and the ability to survive ice ages, but went extinct. Humanity let them down. Scientists, like burglars, use the next drainpipe to plant data in the learned Journals; in this case, to vindicate extinction. It never stops."

"Forgive me, but can you read? You being an Elephant Seal?"

"Good heavens no. I listen."

"Every extinction punctures the supply chain," I suggested. "Layer upon layer of life, mysterious and supernatural, is disappearing. Extinction is in the air."

"There's no justification for optimism," he replied, nodding.

"You blame Darwin?"

"He conjured up hubris, and indifference. We are brainwashed into accepting extinction as necessary. Like Kali dressed up as the saint of knitting.

"Human life is unravelling under the immense forces of Western greed and atomisation; i.e. the worship of liberal individualism. A paradox, since uniformity is unavoidable."

"Sounds good."

"Not by South Atlantic standards. This is where it gets interesting," he said, gobbling up an amuse-bouche of seaweed and sea lice. "Let me tell you, I've always had an interest in Empires. They are big and violent, like me. But also efficient at moving best practice across the world. The opposite of the Galapagos. Without best practice, the outliers are left behind, poisoning others, like Isis, for example."

"Genocide in the Americas was down to measles, smallpox, or flu, wasn't it?" I suggested. "Looked at in that way, Empires are the disease."

"No, that's illogical. It is the absence of Empire which causes mayhem. Empires improve stability. They unify. They create more profound evolution than Western profligacy does. At the microlevel, they improve science, supply chains, control global finance (ask the USA), share knowledge, set boundaries. Far from the deeps of gerrymandering, they had the capacity to raise humanity to new heights. But because they exported religion, and dismissed freedoms as nest-feathering, they lost momentum."

"They bully."

"Get your facts right. Firstly, China is an Empire, not a country. Russia is a country, not an Empire (like Britain). True to form, America opposes Empire, but is, of course, a covert and entrenched Empire itself, their vast scale the result of theft, conquest, buy-outs, – but modified by destabilisation, invasion and cheap and cheerful manipulation. This version of hegemony is not won in fair fight, but imposed massively and cruelly. Ask South Americans, ask socialists. But, like Goebbels, they won the war of words. What sheer size has done for them, they pretend can be achieved by demo-crazy everywhere."

"The Africans?"

"The people left behind complain. The best Empires were based on trade and sea power, not Napoleon."

"Ah, that's special pleading."

"No, no, hear me out. Militarism and dictatorship spawn terrible legacies."

I tapped my nose. "So colonialism spread democracy?"

"Colonialism spread viticulture, the novel, the arms trade, something called cricket, and democracy, yes. Not demo-crazy. Colonialism spread from Greece to Marseilles, from Scotland, to ~Darien. The British were interested in grubby trade much of the time. Trade became the mother of contention."

"But Russia and China won at dictatorship and genocide. British colonies subsequently preferred democracy, as the moderate road to freedom and equality of sorts."

He laughed loudly.

"America has an interest in attacking imperial straw men to distract attention from their venality, e.g. imposing demo-crazy on Africa, Vietnam, Iraq, Afghanistan; but not on Saudi. If you ever study the casualties of the Iraq War, you find few Americans; but enormous numbers of Iraqis, most of them civilians, died. This qualifies by post-modern terms as genocide.

"Moreover, the habit of importing cheap labour from any quarter embroils them in foreign arguments they have difficulty in understanding.

"The British, incapable of ideology (bar Christianity and Queen Victoria, Impress of India), imposed terms of trade, as, of course, do America, along with the ideology of greed.

"Anyway, the Americans claim they have good leaders, who just happen to have access to loadsa dosh. What a coincidence. Animals select leaders according to genetics and hormones. This creates stability. When we need a new leader, we depose an old one, without ceremony. What the world needs is stability, long-term solutions to long-term problems, and a planet nurtured not raped."

Ursula interrupted. "I know both World Wars were caused by the British Empire. I was told so by an Irish American.

"Refugees, in waves, hungry and diseased, Irish, English, Scots, Welsh, Germans, flooded the world. Is this what they mean?

"It reminds me of locusts who are solitary and, when solitary, harm nobody. But hunger draws them to cluster on vegetation. Then they undergo dramatic change. They drop the solitary bit and seek each other's company, developing big muscles and hairy legs. They don't intend harm, but they cause it. The Irish, English, Scots and Welsh didn't intend harm. Some were certainly feckless and violent, and played a disproportionate role in enforcing Imperial rule. This included the killing of aboriginals.

"The strange behaviour of locusts is associated with increases of serotonin.

"Hungry people have low levels of serotonin, and this can express itself in anger and aggression. Quite unfairly, Irish immigrants to the USA were looked down on, because of drunken and antisocial behaviour. Poor serotonin has been associated with increased alcohol consumption.

"There is very little in Darwin's thinking to explain the role of serotonin in locusts."

"But the West is blamed for many of the world's ills," I said.

"Leaders everywhere are wary of the West. Hitler and Napoleon slaughtered Russians. Russians demand a right of reply. *When will the next plague come out of the West?* they ask. And here we go again. Europeans wearing Nato colours, not paid for, march up to the front door again.

"The difference between the West and the rest is the West's unbridled appetites. The reason is demo-crazy. Take food. Americans over-eat. There is no mass hunger, but they swarm around McDonald's. The benefit of vegan diets is incredible. Problems of degradation, extinction, and war would abate. But the democratic West will never agree to it. My species, the Elephant Seals, would benefit. Putin would mandate vegan diets. Xi would. Modi would. The West never. Never.

"Same goes for population control. Excess population causes malnutrition. The appalling harm that malnutrition causes can only be reduced by coercion. But never in democracies. The genus *Pinnipedia* would benefit wildly if killing us was stopped."

"I don't want to argue with you," I interjected. "But can we discuss revolution?"

"Revolution is delusional," he answered. "Liberty is not an absolute and must be parsed. Try explaining that to an American. Americans take it on themselves to distribute their deeply flawed justice around the world. Bush taught Putin how to go to war in defiance of international law. Bush identified Ukraine as the next killing field. Thanks, Bush."

"Do you support Polar Bears?"

"I am no admirer of Polar Bears. They eat seals. This must cease."

"They colonise ice floes. But without colonialism, the whole world would be like Russia. I kid you not," said Ursula. "When the Ottoman Empire collapsed, it gave birth to an endless cycle of awful dictatorships.

"Central Africa is an undemocratic disaster zone, thanks to Belgium. It is the French, the British, and the Dutch who abolished slavery, which existed for Millennia. Of course, it still goes on hale and hearty in China, India, Africa, and the Middle East, under a different lexicography. America is hooked on the next best thing: immigrants, despised and uncontrolled. The British legacy is pluralism, free trade, fair play, respect for minorities, socialism. These are destroying the planet."

"How?"

"They circumvent coercion. Annie says coerce humans or Nature will be destroyed."

"Animals must avoid democracy," said Pericles. "What do you think Democracy is anyway? In America, there is no Demos, therefore no Democracy. A Demos must be capable of an agreement. The Chinese Communist Party is a Demos. USA is a Crazy without a Demos," he chortled.

"How so?" I asked.

"The two main parties in America don't talk," he said. "So much hatred."

"Like Guyana," I suggested. "One group is Indian, one African. Call that democracy? Gridlock and hostility, caused by Britain."

"The Americans have the identical problem. One party, Democrat. One, Republican. Two different ideas. But is real life so binary? Democracy invents differences at the expense of progress. The Chinese have a Big Long-Term Idea. The CCP reduces inefficient differences. Clever."

"Less Gridlock?"

"Exactly. More long-term. Democracy is a joke to intelligent animals," said the Professor. "It over-promises freedoms. Narcissism."

I intervened. "Islam," I said, "has what it takes to protect Nature. China's core competence is brainwashing. The CCP provides the framework, skills and CV for coercion.

"The West needs to tighten freedoms in keeping with a coercive mandate. Let's keep out of China.

"These facts put humans back in their box. Humans," he said, "are as natural as plastic particles."

"I like silent fields," I replied. "I am happy if I see a solitary bee at the end of the tunnel."

"Have you heard of The Ancient of Days?" the elephant seal enquired. "An old bearded man, stark bollock naked, stiff with unkempt hair, uses golden compasses to seek the mean 'twixt man and nature. You, Mr Heeb, could be that man."

"'What the hammer? What the chain? In what furnace was thy brain?' he chanted. Blake painted the Whale, striped green and purple, and the Serpent dancing to the charmer's wand."

Satin looked ridiculously pleased.

The Professor intoned:

"Belle d'abandon

On dirait un serpent qui danse

Au bout d'un baton."

"What does that mean?" we asked.

"A serpent from the deep partnered Samael, who created the earth. Blake was a revolutionary. I, too, am revolutionary," he sighed.

"I'm a revolutionary myself."

"Revolution," said the Professor, fast out of the blocks, "slows to an embouteillage de merde. I have an open mind like a sphynx, and a bottom with a magic sphincter. I will be autocrat, fast and decisive," he said brightly.

"How about fomenting revolution in the USA?" I said.

"The USA was revolting at its inception. Many colonists, not least Britons, were trigger-happy guys looking to line their pockets. Racism ran so deep, it became their biggest export. The Founding Fathers wanted as many goodies as they could get. After all, Jefferson was an indebted slave owner whose motto, 'All men are created equal', defines democracy as hypocrisy, i.e. hypocracy."

"You prefer totalitarianism?"

"I don't need to. Let's just say humans get by comfortably with less. The US Presidency depends on money, definitely unlaundered. Every President since the War smells of it. The old, the degenerate, the younger, sexually unpleasant, corrupt, and inexperienced. Kruschev ran rings round Kennedy, until the Russians lost their nerve. Bobby held secret meetings with the Russkies to fix elections. Makes Trump look like an amateur. Nothing new under the sun, they say.

"To cap it all, these Presidents teach pseudo-democracies how to terrorise each other."

"What should we do, then?" I asked.

"Nature is our paradigm. Complex. Symbiotic. My Vice will be a fungus."

"And our Supreme Court?"

"Sequoias pollarded by gene editing never to compete with politics."

"Will you please lead our Revolution?"

"No. Revolution must have as little diversity as possible, so that rules the Zoo out. Demo-crazy pretends to be disruptive but is very short-term, and devoted by the glib to increasing diversity, because that way lie more votes. Imagine making an agreement with that.

"Revolution promises but does not deliver equality. Women are a kind of litmus test. Women mapped onto male roles appears to achieve some kind of Equality. But Equality is a condition of the soul. Opportunity starts with family, which is the philosopher's stone: a synthesis of genes, culture, parental achievement, and chance. To discount family is to weaken the bonds which uphold morality, and the law: in short, society. That's how you got where you're at. Ask China."

"Equality is a scam," said Ursula, "so now they have invented equity."

Everyone fell silent at this.

"If somebody loses out," she said, "don't pay them damages, help them. Unlike the British, we Germans renounced our past."

"To summarise," said Pericles, "America boasts equality, but is built on inequality. To trump it all, ethnic hurdles are baked in, to make them work twice as hard."

Later, Pericles appointed a steering committee, which I attended. He avoided the topic of Revolution. Elephant seal males can grow to five tons. They mate with fifty, even a hundred wives. They are hyper, but Walruses have bigger dicks.

Undemocratic, rank and violent, Pericles is our Beach Master. I decided to work with him.

"I am the measure of all things," he says, as he sinks into fat, at risk of suffocation, then theorises about theriocracy, the rule of one animal over others. He is lonely and reactionary.

"I am proud," he announces, "to defend the history of my species in the South Atlantic. Our brightest cows mate with small, inferior males way out at sea. Does it justify changing my politics? Never. They want to dispossess me as Beach Master, and dispense with honour, loyalty, and truth. Their stale idea is promiscuity. Tomorrow, some other fad will replace it. Anyway, cows are attracted to power. I won my place in bloody battle."

"So what do we do?" I wondered.

Came his answer: "WAR!"

"We need war," he announced, "or there is no guarantor of safety for women and children. When Ukraine was invaded, women and children fled, as their protection is different to, and more important than, human rights, international law, or identity politics. Politics were invented for males making war, not for seeding binary dissent. Mis-sold equality requires fifty percent of every role in England to be female. Similarly, fifty percent of every role in Guyana would be ethnically based. If the Taliban institutes democracy, will the Amiral Mu'minin be female?

"As Bingo says, when you board the plane, no-one wants the pilot to be a quota beneficiary. This is metaphor.

"By war we prevent population bottlenecks, which destroy genetic diversity, and therefore Nature itself. Geneticists have found evidence of past bottlenecks in humans, doubtless self-inflicted.

"I like to examine these questions through the lens of sex. That is to say dimorphism," he said, breathing more heavily than was nice.

"Bonking is the font of Elephantine life. Young males approaching puberty hang out with alpha bulls. This keeps sexual fantasies in check. Once fully grown, they take turns shagging anything that moves. Each goes on musth in his season; i.e. berserk, breaking the rules, challenging the top males and having the girls in season. Result: optimal exchange of genes, and heightened experiences.

"But alpha males maintain order. I do not wage war to crush my sexual adversaries. I subdue the females. War brings out the flaunt in them.

"I have to hold a cow quite still for the eternal seconds of consummation. I gently hold her head in my enormous mouth, though sometimes… *crack*."

We did not know what to say.

"But cows do not complain. As far as they know, I have a prostate, and a perfectly good todger, but due to the scarcity of mirrors in here, I can't see it. I could tip a bus and would be very happy so to do.

"In my imagination," he said, "I skip into the ocean for a snack. But every second I absent myself, one of my wives is given a seeing to by some five-hundredweight shrimp. How can you have such paradoxes? I am a firm believer in one male having forty votes, to offset the ratio of one vote for each of forty wives. I'm surprised polyandrous humans don't do the same. Otherwise, inequality.

"In many species, the female is more immunocompetent than the male. In immunosuppressive females, Testosterone lengthens their lifespan. Males can't do that. How do the forces of post-modernism square with that? Females who outlive males will, by definition, have more votes than their husbands. This is unfair and will lead to shrinking populations. The females should be disqualified or the votes of males reweighted.

"Females tend to be larger when males are congenitally promiscuous. How big is your wife? Big females dominate. So, in Anglerfish, males end up as rudimentary little squirts with stunted digestive systems. They live off females parasitically. Is this what girls want? It leads to prurient daydreams. Even more elegantly, the Sacculina inject themselves into their females and produce semen, like little elves, but are, in fact, no more than sperm-producing cells in their beloved's gigantic body. Quite romantic really.

"How do you compute equality from that?" he asked. "Can we not intervene with intelligent design?

"In spiders, fecundity is linked to female body size. The males are even titchier and have to avoid female cannibalism by being so small as to not even constitute a snack, and so quick they escape post-coitum like little rockets.

"And then again, some fish change sex only when, and only if, there is no dominant male around. This is deemed fashionable in certain quarters. How do you define politics in such fluidity? The answer has yet to be determined."

"Thank you, Professor, I said. "You could not have been more eloquent."

"I could," he said. "Females do not dream of raping males on my watch. The bigger I get, the more cows I have to do. It's a fine line, I admit." He burped. "My real joy is to swim so deep I can feed in silence and in privacy. If young males dream of fathering children, we must never tilt the world against them, or revolution follows. Does that help?"

"If animals want revolution, my colleague, Annie, has suggested we consult the CCP. My reservation is that the Chinese not only swallowed Marx whole, but Pavlov, too. Under Mao, this led to brainwashing on an industrial scale."

"My plan is to declare war full stop. If China is excluded by the rest of humanity, then, yes, they might make possible allies. That is Alpha logic."

"A rapprochement with Xi requires brainwashers be brainwashed," I murmured.

Satin came back in. "What do the Chinese believe?" she asked. "Will they restore standards?"

We looked at her with new respect.

"Like what?"

"Well, strength, ferocity, guaranteed minima of food and sleep," she suggested.

"Is this what we are looking for?"

"I know what you mean," the Professor responded. "Ban alcohol. You can't abolish the gestalt, but extirpate immorality. Profound."

"You need massive resource, and total obedience, if you choose war."

"Think shoals and flocks," he replied. "They have teams of septuple players, who, sharing with other septuples, form septagons, robust, yet flexible enough to allow huge flocks to spin, reverse, incline at will."

"Whose will? Starlings? Sardines?"

"Exactly," said the Professor.

"The point is: the animal kingdom rarely suffers from organisational dogma."

"No," I said. "Start with animal rights, which trump human rights; children's rights, which trump promiscuous adults; rights for the Natural world, which trump capitalists. Human Rights are a nightmare, in a zero sum game which we are losing. Let's get the Chinese to take a lead. If children and the wild are at the back of the queue, you disenfranchise the future."

"I am not interested in rights," said the Professor. "I am interested in clean things, dominance and survival. If you make autonomy the criterion for recreation, abortion, and exclusion, you damage life. Autonomy is another word for selfishness.

Nature loomed beyond the ken of the pineal gland as it squints into iPhones and computer games, blind to reality. High above a chestnut tree I saw a shadow fall, like a vast bird, hawking. Plumb down it dropped, intent on ending all that lived in the soft green grass below, amongst flowers and bees. It swooped. It outran gravity. So dark, its mystery made the lands shimmer with life. Nothing like this had I seen in Russia.

"I feel awe at mystery and power in Nature. Especially at night, when our sense of hearing and imagination are sharpened, Nature calls urgently. If we are lucky, we respond."

I had a left over from the gift sent to me by Eleniya's people. I took it.

"Men," Circe says, "cry pitifully for relief, due to unrealistic childhood promises. Hence Incels. I know what triggers sex in animals, but not humans. Is it blood flow?"

Satin winked at me.

"Not enough attention has been paid to men who can't attract partners in the first place," I volunteered.

"Love is symbiotic," interjected Annie.

"Well, yes. Or is it synechdochic? Or synostosic? Synaesthesic? Sin comes in somewhere."

He laughed unnaturally. It was not long afterwards that we lost Snag. He felt we were too soft, too compromising, and left us.

Satin is confused about love. Little does she know, it is a hall of mirrors. Circe is tender towards Major Sausage, but she calls the shots. "There are rules," she says. "The weak must have precedence. That is what post-modernism means.

"Because of our emotional supremacy, women rule by consensus," she said. "Engineers, male, process-obsessed, try to override emotional intelligence."

Circe turned on Annie. "Atheists," she said, "hate their fathers. Freud's was a pervert. Diderot usurped his. Voltaire did not like God too close."

"My father," said Annie, "is different. He is proud of my relationship."

This came as a shock.

"Poets are escapists," jeered Circe. "Real lovers just get on with it."

"Elephants," countered Annie, "are supreme mothers, as is Snow White. They're borrowing a Grizzly to get Snow White pregnant."

"She'll take down any Grizzly."

"Hyena females, like Bonobos, have clitorises the size of door knobs. They're alpha females."

"It's Alpha males which are violent," Circe replied. "Chimp males attack Gorillas, even kill their young. They hunt Bonobos, eat them. Evil evolves in males. My mother was involved in the Great Ape Project. Apes were not to be detained except in their own interests."

I leave, thinking Annie has definitely gone potty. I had tried a substance used to induce hibernation. This stimulates adenosine receptors in the brain. The markings on the container had been memorised by some friendly creature. Long story short, I fell into a dream. Some sort of syncope.

I visit the poison dart frogs in their green livery, as they eye me toxically. Like jewels, they incite me to touch them, and die. Lapis Lazuli frogs; Selenite moon-faced frogs; Moldovia frogs, blue-black with a poisonous ring about their heads. What does this mean? Have I gone off piste. As a fart, some might say?

Satin wants her confinement in human form. She is over-confident.

"Try to face facts," I said. "It is safer to go into labour fit and strong."

"It's not my nature to talk of risks. I do not think like that," she growled.

"While you know no fear, I am terrified. But my admiration of you knows no bounds."

"You and I have an agreement. Will you stand by me?" she demanded.

"If you have problems at childbirth, what then? Have you had a scan? How many foetuses do they predict?"

"Only three."

"How many would a Jaguar expect?"

"Two. I am a Jaguar."

"I don't understand."

"You will end up the father of wild animals," she warned. "How long before you look down on us?"

She changed her mind, of course. The birth was simple. Somehow, there were three cubs. Their eyes would not open. Their mother licked them into life. The third died, which made me cry. Satin spent no time with the small dead body. I felt a dull pain over my heart.

The survivors mewed as their mother's tongue revived them, extraordinary in the rough shape of the papillae.

The newborns suckled in a determined way. Mesmerised, I felt a powerful attachment.

I spoke in an urgent whisper to their mother, but she ignored me.

What astonishes me is the excitement in the Zoo. Greeted with wonder, they portend the beginning of a new and hopeful era.

For medicinal reasons, Satin was briefly absent. Ulysses put the cubs in a monstrous big pram and took them on a tour, affording the animals a glimpse of the celebrities. Some, like Anita, gazed on with sadness. The horses shied. The hyenas crowded their fence, menacingly.

But widespread support suggests love of the newborn is a force transcending species.

When the caravanserai passed, Pericles looked on haughtily. He trampled his offspring in the crowded colonies of his youth. But I saw his tender gaze.

After the cubs were returned to their mother, she sniffed them suspiciously, and refused to recognise me. I knew now war was coming.

I love watching her suckling. Whenever she is removed from the enclosure, I try to play with them. Sacrifice plays on my mind.

Do cubs have souls? This is where I part company with Annie. It is obvious to me that men are animals writ in a strange script. She thinks humans superior to other life-forms.

I had to have things out with Pericles.

"I know you have set your mind against revolution," I said, "but…"

"A successful revolution requires a big idea. We don't have one," he replied.

"How about 'saving the Rainforests'?"

"Who is going to risk life for that?"

"Stop globe warming, then?"

"Revolutions are based on faulty premises. Poor Stalin had to kill his entourage. The Germans had to lose two wars before America would reward them. America promised the earth to the Shia, the Vietnamese, Mobutu. I could go on."

I was invited to drinks by Annie's dad.

Greeted at his front door, I noticed his tummy bulging over an old school tie. He was wearing two, one around his neck, the other holding up his trousers.

"Ah, Heeb," he said. "Nice of you to come. I hear good things about you. Do you play golf? Drake plays off seven. Not too shabby."

"Sadly, I don't have time."

"Pity," he said, somehow contracting his nose so the word came out as if brought up from the cellar to connote superiority. "Our club is the greatest in all England. Now, I want to introduce you to a personal friend, Clementine. She has insights into the animal kingdom." He expelled a hiss from behind his teeth, suggesting a private joke, destined to remain so.

"Clemmie," he said, "this is Heeb, you've heard so much about."

"You must be very special to have Annie on your team," she said.

She was beautiful, in a way. There was neither divinity nor animality on show. Her face, narrow and fine, suggested fragility, nerves, condescension.

"How brave to take on the human race," she said in a dark voice.

"Oh?" I blinked. "Am I an outsider?" I tried my most winning smile.

Somehow, the room emptied. She was confiding in me, but very, very softly. I drew closer.

"Her father is disquieted by Annie's lifestyle," she breathed. "All that idealism. She works too hard."

"We do."

"Strange things happen with terrible effects. Do you dabble in social media?"

"Can't say I do."

"Are you aware of the unsavoury gossip about the zoo? A Polar Bear?"

"I am on the outside looking in. I have other fish to fry," I replied.

"How modest. From a great distance it seems exciting. A Silovarch? Fanciful tales? Drug-taking? I know. Annie is taken by your horticultural knowledge? Brugmansias? Animal communication?"

"I assure you, Annie and I just work our socks off trying to raise money for the rainforests."

"Let's ask her," she said in a high voice, capturing everyone's attention.

"Annie, dear, this lovely man has detoxified the Zoo. I feel let down. What were you telling me?"

"Oh, tittle tattle," Annie replied defensively.

"Do you know Con O'Divoleen?" asked Clementine. "Do you read the *Daily Truss*? A reporter, but just a decent, local boy. He tells me he is about to lift the lid on your Zoo."

"Do tell. Are we doing wrong?"

"Not you. Not you. But we are anxious for dear Annie. Is she necessary to your project?"

"I am afraid she is."

"I am," said Annie, "at full stretch doing things for a Prince."

"As for the *Daily Truss*, I understand the scoop is photographic."

I winked at Annie. She looked displeased.

"Now tell me, Mr Heeb," continued Clementine, "do you have a handle on the psycho-spiritual implications of your work?"

"Not really. I am very old school. My guru is Sir Alistair Hardy, who was a scientist and Christian both."

"Zoogmatically?"

"Yes. Ha, ha. He loved to tell how marsupial and mammals, properly placental mammals, evolved simulacra of each other. Another conundrum. You can't just say the environments were similar. Surely?"

"I have a Hardy first edition with his signature," she said. "I must show you. May I extend an invitation to you both? A drink? A bookfest?"

Annie smiled. "Clementine thinks our project is a waste of time. She is an atheist. Unlike my Prince."

"England has long held that men have souls, has it not?" she said. "Maybe unfashionable, but uncontroversial. The Chinese who think of forging heaven on earth, incarcerate eccentrics by diagnosing Zoochosis."

"Isn't that racism?"

"Just communism. Pavlov, you may remember, rang a bell and made dogs dribble. But he went further. He applied his theories to humans. The communists took him seriously. In short, they set Pavlov upon man. Deprived us of sleep, food, self-belief. Enough stress and we break."

"Guantanamo?" she said.

"I can't say. The liberal media equate Western misrepresentation with the vile atrocities inflicted in the name of Lo Jui-ching."

I rose to the bait. "Pavlov," I said, "identified the kind of humans who are incapable of withstanding brainwashing. Like the Ipcress filer. Russia and China worked hard at breaking the deplorables utterly, not infrequently disposing of them. But look, in a cast of billions, such misjudgements may not amount to much. Put it another way: if we could sell Marxism to America, we might resuscitate the planet. But my heart is with those destroyed by Pavlov. Take a long spoon."

My colleagues see humans as imperfect but precious, capable of unspeakable courage, tenderness and deep, deep love. The first step to decadence is intellectuals who arbitrage truth.

"Do we know when we have sinned?" asked Clementine.

Annie thinks tyranny, even war, is preferable to revolution.

Annie came over. "We are the authors of ourselves," she said. "Truth, law, morality are all subjective. That's why they keep changing. To save Nature, we need red lines, we need stability, not unfettered capitalism."

"But pity demands the intervention of science and poetry. Then we can claim authority and reject the old ideas," said Clementine.

Instantly, I saw what they had done. They made the subjectivity of humans and so-called autonomy a wall against revolution. This drives me mad. She is putting Nature at risk. She ignores morality.

"To save Nature, don't we need religion?"

Clemmie smiled. Annie scowled.

"Scientists are half as likely to be religious as the wider population," I said. "Popular opinion replaces religion, when Darwin explains life, competition extinction, everything."

"Culture does not change in an orderly fashion," she said. "But life improves with adaptation."

"Like detergents in the supermarket? No-one needs to pay attention? What goes extinct has no value. The forests burn, the tigers and elephants are trapped or killed. The horn is amputated with a buzzsaw from the living rhino. Progress.

"Tears are shed," Annie concluded. "Creon has to forbid Antigone."

Later, I wondered: was Darwin really to blame? He turned his back on religion. The sublime truth is that man is subject to a higher order of reality – not unproven beliefs of here-today-absent-tomorrow scientists. Yet Darwin was sold on perfectibility.

Men are just beings, while the symbiosis of a trillion billion creatures create untold innovation. I announced this to everyone at her dad's cocktail party, after one gin too many. But, of course, creation is an outmoded concept.

Now earth and all life on it are in danger. Darwin's theory of extinctions was not based on information. Convinced that evolution happens very slowly, he did not know about the big five extinctions when seventy-five percent of diversity disappeared. He had a poor understanding of the environment. As far as I can see, he leaves little room for plasticity, or epigenetics, or even, surprisingly, mutations. Some ascribe to him ideological certainty on such matters. The problem is science. In their greenhorn way, they invested in Darwin so ecstatically, they invented a great general who defeated the church. They lost face.

Annie's father bearded me. "I forbid you to use that word 'evolution' in my house. It just means the opening of a book. I am coining a new word: Endokainosis, Not Anakainosis, as St Paul used it, to mean renewal of the mind. But Endokainosis, meaning renewal of life from within."

Annie's dad is a Christian, which explains why she's an atheist. But his suggestion that we describe life in an ancient language sums him up.

"If we are gunned down by a germ, a car, or a catastrophe," he continued, "we cease to exist. But if our infant is different to all other infants, a great act of innovation has taken place, not in the wild, not in hand-to-hand combat with competitors, but from within. Endokainosis."

"Perhaps we need to undo Darwin?" I suggested.

"Why not?"

There and then I warmed to him. "Find a better magus?" I said. "A woman, perhaps?"

"The biologist Lynn Margulis, famous for her work on endosymbiosis, might have been the ticket, though a smidgeon rebellious," he replied.

"She contended symbiosis is a driving force behind life on earth."

"Didn't she consider Darwin's notion of evolution to be insufficient?"

"She claimed co-operation, interaction, and mutual dependence among organisms shaped the world. Life did not take over the globe by combat," Annie said, "but by networking."

"That is a bit far-fetched."

"All that is left to do is exorcise Darwin," I suggested. "The way to modify behaviour is by revolution. We need to win the argument."

"Archaeologists can tell what humans killed, by butchers' marks upon the bones. Most predators kill the old, or very young, the ill, the lame. Not man. From the beginning, he hunted everything that had the temerity to exist. That's what butchery reveals.

"By choosing to adopt totems, and obey God, mankind may yet come to love Nature."

I put this to Annie. "Can you imagine the Chinese adopting compassion?"

"I think they do," she said.

This conversation marked a step change in Annie's confidence. At our next meeting, she gave a sort of speech. "The future is hiding in the past. Global Warming hastens famine," she proclaimed.

"Human famine, right?"

"We talk of Russian and Chinese famines as if they started something new. Stalin's famine was in 1932-3, but

Russian famines killed a good deal less than the Indian subcontinent suffered under the British, from Doji Bara to the Second World War, over which period the East India Company and then the British Empire must take responsibility. Mao's famine from 1958-62 ran at twice the number of those deaths over a fraction of the years involved. That is what I call extinction. We must learn from all three and from Africa and Ireland."

"I'm sure Mao studied Malthus. Darwin did. Trevelyan did at Haileybury," said the Major.

"Trevelyan?"

"He administered famine in Ireland and India. Mao and Trevelyan were alike, accepting and belatedly cutting immense losses."

"Mao knew best?"

"Famine in China was apocalyptic, yet, to him, cyclical, and a fact of life. He applied the half-glass-full test. 'If we lose three hundred million, the survivors will ensure victory,' he said. It is better to let half die so the other half may eat their fill."

"His glass-half-full of bureaucrats, arse-lickers, and credulous youngsters?" jeered the Major.

"You don't want Mao on our team?"

"He intuited the survivors would esteem him," Annie continued, "but not the dead, of course. Central Asia still esteems Stalin. The Chinese Communist Party controls the army, the police, the courts, the media. They understand control."

"But not famine?"

"That's not fair," she complained. "When they wanted to slow down the birth rate, they took action. The West wonders why they never reviewed the Great Leap Forward. But the Chinese knew very well the scale, losses, patterns, and moved on."

"Bad decisions!"

"Many cruel. But they know coercion. We do not." Annie sounded apologetic.

"The British never learned from the Irish famine?" I asked.

"That's true. The Chinese and the British have something in common. Malthus argued for the betterment of survivors, consigning others to their fate. In Britain, progress based on never-ending struggle seemed to justify an admixture of morality, belief, and prejudice. The British intervened to reduce death, but insisted on private trade taking the strain for much of what would now pass to the State. That was Trevelyan, of Haileybury, Ireland, and India.

"Now, once again, Famine, the grim apocalyptic spectre, appears on the horizon. Darwin saw in Malthus a rationale for extermination, and a catalyst of new forms. Thence comes the idea of extinction of inadequate species. The politics permit laziness. The working class must adapt. Nature must take care of itself. Further loss of biodiversity is inevitable. Science will slow the process, even reverse it.

"The Chinese are on a different plane. If any nation can take on global warming, they can. The CCP, the party, is dictator. It lends its power to the leader, who consults popular opinion, then decides and does not waiver," said my Annie. She had made up her mind.

"What did we think of Mao, Annie?"

"Hot topics back then were abortion, race riots, the bomb, subliminal advertising, attempts to save the British car industry."

"How does the BBC see things now?"

"Covid, Ukraine Trans, inflation. Famine must work its socks off to displace Feast."

"What is important now?"

"Mental health. TV ads offer instant relief against cruelty to pets."

At this stage, poor Annie had no idea who Professor Pericles was.

"I have not met him," she said. "Heebie, I keep getting reports of you stopping in front of enclosures and making animal noises, as if trying to communicate with them."

"I do," I said. "I do." I laughed wildly.

"I'm told this Professor is going to change the Mission Statement. More ESG, I gather," she said, while passing me a note which simply read: 'I am in love with you.'

She loves me if she must, I thought. She needs love to flow through her. I pity her. But that is not the greatest of my concerns.

Then Satin disappeared, putting our young at risk.

My children now had to suckle at a Sow. Feeling tired and sad, I went in search of the Professor.

When I found him, he demanded a Senior Independent Director draw up a succession plan.

"It's not clear there is anyone as clever as me," he said.

"Who are the candidates?"

"The snake – Hissing SID, I call him. By the way, the animals want you dead."

I was now cooking up a nervous breakdown. Why was I here at all? Perhaps because Britain is at the epicentre of mining, slavery, famine, industrialisation, transportation, indentured labour, and is expected to purge the evils it has caused.

Of course, the real action is in South America. Some constitutions are even worse than America's. If the Ministry of Agriculture is the plaything of the land-owning classes with a vested interest in turning the Rainforest into beef, the Amerindian population is terrorised. If the Ministry of Agriculture defines where the indigenous may live, they can forcibly relocate them, along the lines of Stalin. Presidents attack the natives for their ignorance. More than two hundred environmentalists and seventy-four human rights activists have given up their lives in the defence of the rainforest. "This," says Pericles, "is a democracy in which the Demos trample the weak and the oppressed. This will drag them back to slavery. It suggests democracy contains in its DNA such mutations as wickedness, a malign complacency, a decadence, and a propensity for corruption and internecine feuding.

"We, say the democrats, have a failsafe way of replacing bad government. But they don't. The next party will promise the unaffordable; and the opposition will cry foul and get back in again. Why? To bleed Nature in order to win votes.

"The foolishness of Dictators, you say. And you have a point. But the British Empire, under-resourced and light touch, subcontracted regional government to the East India Company. This is typical of democracy intent on fostering wealth, looting votes, and failing to contain famine.

"So, do you prefer Trevelyan or Mao? Democrat or autocrat? In a world where Nature is besieged."

"Autocracy," I concede, "is an incubus that rapes and smothers sleeping victims, the old, the innocent. Autocrats, by their hold on grain, oil, gas, and vital raw materials, strangle their opponents. They export inflation, which others are unable to resist. So democracies become unhinged."

Annie hides behind democracy and promises coercion. "If we do not favour Nature, Nature herself will turn hyperinflationary," she insists.

Meanwhile, I decided to keep my own counsel. I contacted Eleniya's father and asked him to help me find a Shaman.

He suggested a Korean. Sadly, I know nothing of Shamanism in Korea. But I am confident that Shamans everywhere seek balance and respect for Mother Earth, just as Taoism fosters Earth's harmony.

They put me in touch with a Khaka woman, and I find the money to go out and meet her.

As soon as I arrive, I organise a photoshoot, and she very kindly dresses up in her regalia, which includes magnificent fish owl feathers. She also dug up some paraphernalia, including a bear's claw which was photogenic.

Conversation is positive.

"I am thirty thousand years old," she says, "much older than other religions. Eleniya left a great legacy. We believe the spirits of the wild are nourished by her death."

I must have looked shocked, for she holds my hand.

"I know you follow a tree totem," she says, "and you want to drive out an evil spirit. Tell me, who is this demon? And who is the poor soul who suffers under him?"

"The poor soul is a zoo keeper, and his name is Ulysses."

"And what is the evil spirit that possesses him?"

"It is the old Demon of Extinction."

"And does this zoo keeper want the demon driven out of him?"

"No. He does not understand."

"Then you are asking too much. My powers cannot be taken lightly."

"But if you and your helpers hold a ceremony to banish this spirit, will that not suffice?"

"I think not. But I can try, in remembrance of Eleniya. The modern way is never to drive out a spirit if the possessed is suffering from a disorder like hysteria, psychesthenia, or trauma."

"Oh, nothing like that."

"That's OK, then. And no secondary personalities?"

"None at all. No, no. The guy is in the best of mental health."

"What is the name of this demon?"

"CR Darwin. If you draw up a questionnaire, I will take it back to England and get any information you need."

"I know you have a close friend amongst the animals. One who may be a Shaman?"

"Who?" I ask.

"The name of a Shaman is taboo, as the name of God is taboo in these new religions."

"Did you know I was hunting when I last came to the Taiga?"

"That is all right. Hunting is a pure activity, perhaps the oldest thing humankind has practised. Every single step the hunter takes must respect the hunted animal and the spirits of the forest. The spirits of the water and the forest are offended if the hunters desecrate. They must follow our rituals."

"Did Eleniya worship Mother Earth? May I pay my respects?"

"Yes, of course. Did you know the dry land was created by the Golden Eye in the beginning?"

"That must have been millions of years ago. Is that possible?"

"Time is circular. I think you wish to do good to animals."

"Will you come to England, then?"

"That is unnecessary. Provide photographs of the victims, and, if you can, a bit of clothing or hair. We will burn sage and drink a potion. And all will change."

When I got back to England, I explained to Ulysses that I was doing research and asked him to help with the questionnaire.

He proved obstructive, and annoyingly interrogated me as to why I had taken on this project. He hinted at secrets which I was withholding from him. "I know," he said, "you are having an affair."

This was out of keeping with his character. I felt worried.

"Look, let's get this over and done with," I said. "I am putting you down as the respondent. Let me record what you have to say."

"I am in the habit of telling the truth and sticking to it," he said.

Then, in so many words, I asked, "Are you comfortable with your situation here?"

"Of course. Or I would move on."

"So what do you want to achieve?"

"My vocation is to save animals."

"What are you afraid might happen to these animals if left in the wild?"

"They would lose their lives."

"Prematurely."

"Man's higher calling is to act as steward of Nature. If not, yet more go extinct."

"Apart from providing food and medication, what else do you do?"

At this, he seemed to have a problem. His eyes darted this way and that and his expression took on a haggard mien.

"I do everything to look after my animals," he said, giving the impression he was wounded. "I would like to get back to work," he said. "I don't see the point of this."

"Do you not think that science harms the animal kingdom rather than helps it? That scientific theory has harmed Nature?"

"Not in the least. The ancients harmed natural life."

"Do you think Darwin did, too?"

"What rot!" he said.

"That is my last question. One last thing. My Russian friends sent me this pick-me-up. Give it a try and let me have your feedback. I think you will agree, it smells heavenly."

In a devil-may-care way, he took some there and then.

I returned the questionnaire to my Shaman, in the knowledge that Ulysses now detested me.

A week later, I checked my emails to see if Exorcism works remotely.

'It is hard to say,' came the reply. 'For full effect, you need the sound of loud drums, and a small blood sacrifice. I believe you have to hand a tiger.'

So I threw a little party and invited Ulysses. Very loud music proved no problem. Ganja was available. He appeared to be relaxed.

"You've heard I am planning to get Snow White pregnant?"

"She will be a superb mother."

Ulysses laughed.

"Today's mothers," he said, "are called 'birthing people' who 'chest feed' their unsexed infants."

"I hear you're to mate the Polar Bear with a Grizzly. Good luck with that."

"Hybridisation," he proclaimed, "is the future. It can increase variation, reduce reproductive isolation and in the right hands increase innovation. Straight out of Darwin's playbook."

On my way home, the lights from the Zoo played tricks on me. I thought I saw a snake gliding down a tree. It was, I hoped, the sign of successful exorcism.

The next day, dear Attenborough and Packham announced a BBC initiative to include Nature in ESG protocols. Dawkins wrote a foreword.

Chapter Fifteen

Venetsianov's obituary came out in today's paper. I rang the Embassy, but failed to learn anything further. So I went round to Kensington Palace Gardens. They were apologetic and assured me Venetsianov was very well indeed and in a meeting. After a telephone call, they arranged for us to meet for dinner at the Ognisko Poliskie in Princes Gate, of all places.

He appeared punctually and was made a fuss of by the *maître d'*.

"Prince," I hailed him. Maybe in Poland I should call him Majesty.

"It says in your obit you were a great Darwinian," I said, "but now I find you are alive and kicking and looking very, very well."

"Mr Heeb. A pleasure to see you. How is your Darwin?"

"Surprisingly, he has been no-platformed at Shrewsbury, his old school. This makes me think he has somehow been exorcised."

"Yes, yes. He had a mania for walking, so I read."

"I am keen to learn how the forest near Archangel is progressing."

"You can work it out. Tree felling brings in twenty billion US into Orlik's coffers. Illegal logging is commonplace."

"To plant one million trees would cost twenty-five billion US to plant and tend over fifty years in today's money."

"So it will be hard to replenish forests profitably. But your friend Orlik is beating the system."

"Orlik?"

"Gowler. Gowler. He devised a Ponzi scheme. It attracts 'green' investors in the West to rescue the planet. He pretends the savings will come from lower emissions, and from more effective regulation. He promises all this will be crystallised in every Western pension."

"Is he doing the right thing?"

"I hoped you would tell me. Does he have a good character?"

"He told me once he was an Alpha male."

"This is a normal joke told by the top man."

"It means no-one tells the truth. Very wise, very senior men submit to the Alpha. They quickly learn that submission pleases everyone, since it affirms the system is actually working.

"And if he talks down to the submissives, they like that, too."

"So he is pleasing everyone?"

"Not quite. To obtain funding, he oversells, gets over-confident and fails investors."

"Doesn't care?"

"Perhaps feels he doesn't need to."

"Is there a risk?"

"Seeing he does not take people with him save by force, investors lose confidence. It's not that he can't empathise. He just doesn't."

"Does this embarrass you?"

"People do not like him. This does not reflect well on me. But it is out of my hands now. I should have held him back. Now it's all too late. His success means he is in a different sphere."

"Ah, the curse of being Alpha male."

"We have a scientist, Professor Pavel Borisovich, who studies enthusiasms. He told me once that dominance triggers submission, unavoidably. Whole tiers in large organisations become trapped in it."

"Surely the Alpha male can cope?"

"Maybe. But Borisovich likened its lesions to the prefrontal cortex. Alpha males lose the ability to process social hierarchy, its cues, and co-operation."

"Or the inclination."

"Or the inclination. That's why ladies are so important."

"Evolution, I have read, can lead to alpha females in naked mole rats who have permanently elevated testosterone."

The next time I saw the Professor, I noticed he was wearing a chain of office, fashioned out of fish bones. Sucking at them, he made a speech.

"We have reached a terrible moment in world history," he announced. "Man is trapped in an enclosure of his own design, the Human Zoo. Man fails to see that sin leads to his own extinction. Or that, by opposing Nature, he confirms the end of days."

"What can we do?" I enquired.

"War," he replied. "First, I will demand a treaty, to set aside half the Rainforests and half the Oceans as protected zones, administered by a du-umvirate of China and America."

"Or else it's war? On who, exactly?"

"Everyone."

"Why will animals agree?"

"What choice do they have?"

"What's wrong with Revolution?"

"We need international allies to crush humanity."

As if in answer, came a proposal from the Secretary General to protect rainforests and biodiversity.

"This is the Chinese kicking it into the bamboo," said our Panda.

"Imperialism is encoded in their genes. It's like the tide. Chinese imperialists come and go, then come again. In the past, the Chinese ship of State foundered on the rocks of Korea, then on the shores of Vietnam. Then the Uighars, the Mongols, the Japanese, the Russians, the Arabs, the Turks, the Europeans. They all stopped the Chinese for a little while. Who licked their wounds, took two steps backwards, started again."

"But haven't China changed tack by supporting Russia?"

"Not really. They intend to eat Russia in several helpings."

Then Bingo, that astute old blackguard, broke cover and announced a Biodiversity Festival in London. Simultaneously, a new axis was announced, dedicated to genetic improvement of five crops of geopolitical importance. The axis, unexpected as it was fissiparous, comprised of USA, Canada, Russia, Ukraine, Congo, Indonesia and Malaysia, some of whom were at war with one other. The purpose is to create an OPEC of food. Biodiversity in this context means gene manipulation in the interests of a Cartel of cereal and edible oil producers.

Thanks to my association with Bingo, I was invited to a PR event intended to win hearts and minds.

Bingo got the *FT* to focus on an Indian matrix which was built on Kaushitaki Upanishad. Behaviour in this life apparently determines rebirth in the next. Biodiversity is seeded by using ancient texts to inject spiritualism into the food.

Excellent journalism revealed an extraordinary number of Indian practitioners under investigation.

From the touchline, Circe pointed out that in the Amazon, dead people come back to life as Jaguars, not worms, and that this has been verified by sworn affidavits, etc. She poopoo-ed (etymology French) the idea that men are reborn as insects.

"I thought all men were pigs," I said.

Anyway, we were disappointed. The Trade Mission at the Excel put on a pantomime of rare species.

Sadly, it turned into a lewd showcase of exotic foods. Once again, humans lost the plot. A promised agreement to ban Chinese medicine was revealed as spin.

"The problem," said the Professor, "is that in the absence of collaboration between China and America, nothing happens. Biodiversity must wait."

I attended the Mission's lunch. Like the Cena Tremalchionis, Chinese, Brazilian, and Indonesian food were presented. An Anaconda was cooked in a vast industrial oven. Inside the anaconda was a deer, inside the deer a parrot, and inside the parrot a tiny hummingbird which fainted and stopped humming. Odd, since parrots don't eat hummingbirds. The whole gallimaufry was sliced open and by *trompe l'oeil*, endangered birds were released.

I fell in with a crowd of PR men, Estonians, food buffs and green politicians. Apparently, a plot is underway to divest Bingo.

My last playtime with the twins had been celebrated with hissing, gasping, and even an attempted growl. It now seems an age away. No matter. Fatherhood is achieved with tears and sacrifice.

I think of my home country, where animals become people, and people become animals, neither side realising exactly what they are marrying. Sex in marriage and parenthood are thought most desirable, but in England less so.

England is a small outlier. Across the world, the things we hold dear – the sublime, the influence of nature, the predicate of human life – are under siege. Who to turn to?

Russia and China treat people as expendable. Why? The perverted goal of mind control? The deeply engrained will to dispose of opposition? What we need is revolution, not war, but a revolution of the spirit, with compassion at its heart. In the East, there is a tiny ray of hope. All aspects of Nature are in Tao. Though the idealists in Cheng Feng were crushed, global leadership under China may yet be achieved.

But, sadly, Pericles forbids revolution.

Annie says trees were worshipped in the Andreasweald. Green men and Wodwos, the wild men of the woods, bore witness to this. They worshipped Hengist and made, we are told, obeisance to a stallion. But when Irishmen invaded the West of Scotland, the clans held heather, wild herbs, and flowers to be their totems.

Since then, Nature has been neutered by priesthoods, absentee land owners, capitalists, communists, and, mostly, poets.

By the time Samuel Palmer painted *Shoreham*, the map of paradise was soaked in acid. They imagined Heaven as a pastoral in which tame livestock gathered in nooks and dells; and bathed in the golden light of an unnatural paradise.

Palmer became exercised by the great Reform Bill and the destruction of the pastoral world of his youth. Artists failed to see the great wound in Nature's side, which man violently dealt.

When belief, mystery, worship were known to be treasure, God led the Ancients. But nihilism and materialism, like moths, ate the treasure. The Wild in love's absence is dying, but not yet seen.

Is there, I wondered, a sage in the East who might yet teach us holistic love? Putin and Solzhenitsyn share beliefs. It is cynicism on both sides that divides them. And as for China, where oh where is compassion?

I lived in an oak tree until amidst noises of internal plumbing suggested indigestion. This told me to reunite with my corporeal self. I returned to an airless room. The door was open upon Bingo and a Doctor examining my body.

"Bingo," I cried. "Thank God."

"Have you come back?" he gasped. "We thought you dead."

"An illusion. I am reborn."

"I was tipped off by your colleague, Annie," he explained. "She said you had a turn at the table. She saw them bundle you into a taxi, and out of curiosity she followed and tracked you down. She's a good sort."

"A good sort. I must get to the Zoo. Are the Jaguar's cubs safe?"

"I understand there is a religious ceremony in the Excel at which a Jaguar is to be the Star turn. I am going there myself. Is he OK to go?" Bingo asked the Doctor.

"Oh, yes, good to go."

So we rushed there in an ambulance in time to witness Satin welcomed as a deity.

These events induced in me an abreaction. If there is ever a neutral China, this would expose the falsehoods of the West. Without Chinese help, humanity will avoid coercion, but then Nature will fail. Of course, those of a more parochial mindset argue the Chinese cannot be trusted, as they, like the Russians, have form. Both promoted tyranny, and plan to rule the world.

But the Chinese Communist Party is protean, nimble, willing to adapt, and immensely purposeful.

Pericles continues as our figurehead. He commanded a march past to raise morale. This made it all too clear the Animal Kingdom is unprepared. Rumours circulate that Satin is taking over.

I audited our resources. Could we get a fighting force into the field?

So many ants, we are inexhaustible. Like Putin, but more so.

We managed to track down Kwong and arranged a meeting.

"It was good of you to get back to me," I said. "I need your help."

He took a golden toothpick from its holder. "What can I do for you?"

"I am awe-struck by the progress you are making in gene editing."

"We are."

"I love Wu, so famous in China for using centipede, scorpion, leech and cicada to treat cardiovascular diseases. Are there more such remedies in China?"

"Naturally."

"And herbal remedies for battleground fatigue? My investors wish to put their money into your science. I hear you're working on the current shortage of cashmere. A new strain of Chinese goat, perhaps?

"I remember how you linked Tao to Nature in ways that transform Chinese science."

He ran his golden toothpick up and down the perfect synapses of his teeth.

"And so?" he asked.

"Chinese Medicine is a gateway to evolution, and, forgive me, to profit. Life expectancy, virility. Things the rich will pay for."

"You ask what we will approve?"

"Your scientists are helping animals to withstand global warming, I hear, by increasing the ears, the tails, the legs of animals and birds, the better to regulate their temperatures and prolong their lives. Homeostasis?"

"They do."

"I hear of a Rhinoceros with elephant's ears. And a parakeet with a beak like rhino horn. I'm sure the marketing opportunities have not escaped you?"

"I know."

"I hear of great work afoot to redesign sea snakes. Global warming makes salt water a profitable commodity. Sea snakes inhale oxygen beneath the water. They can be released in domestic sewage and their genes edited for wider assimilation. Can you confirm?"

"You mention medicines for the rich."

"I am fond of pangolins. Around 2.7 million are hunted annually, mostly for the Chinese market. To promote virility?"

"Maybe."

"I also hear a bowl of Tiger soup fetches three thousand US dollars. To cure impotence? Soon, there will be no Tigers. Does that not worry you? Are you impotent?"

"Not really. The rumour is false. There are other cures. Bear bile, for example, is quite good. But that is getting scarce, too," he said. "So many problems. But remember, President Xi has great things to do."

"Maybe the lowly Gecko can help," I said. "But as China gets richer and Chinese medicines dry up, President Xi will see people are dissatisfied. Let me cut to the chase. Help us. We both need tigers, bears, scorpions, centipedes. We need a stream of natural medicines. Can you create new species?"

"What do you have in mind?" he asked, sheathing his little toothpick.

"Snakes?" I said. "But bigger. Giant Scorpions. Amphibious Killer Whales. Vegetarian Tigers, ideally boneless. Rhinos with bigger brains cooled by even more enormous ears."

"I will brief the CCP," he said.

I can hear your exasperation, dear reader. This narrator, you are saying, claims to stand for Nature and its vast heritage. So why is he fantasising?

But the world is changing fast. Annie says China is decisive. The decadent West is tilting against the Wild. Move fast. Or mankind will bring Nature to her knees; and Nature on its knees bites savagely.

Annie says I love religion.

Religion is designed only to please humans. It must be broken. Only then can we reach God.

"So break with the past," says Annie.

"Women once were centre stage," she said. "In Thessaloniki, Christ is depicted as a woman. The gospel according to Mary showed she was closer to Jesus than the men. None of that condones religion. Christ was magnificent when female, until Constantine manned it up. By institutionalising it, he marginalised women once again."

"I don't care. Religion was born anew, wasn't it? Was that not a triumph? Europe became Christian, didn't it?"

"Yes," said Annie ungraciously.

Gaga left a security gate unclosed. Attacked by Snow White, she was rushed to hospital, her right arm permanently damaged.

"I did not expect that," said Ulysses. "I thought terrorism more likely."

"It was terrorism."

"All Snow White can expect now is the humane killer or pregnancy. My Grizzly Bear is big enough to take her. We can study hybridisation."

It was the middle of the night. The animals arranged themselves around Satin's empty enclosure, half-lit by torches made of pitch, which threw a lurid light upon the shadows magnified by wind.

I volunteered to stand shoulder to shoulder with them all.

The flying fox spoke. "All this time, you played with us. I declare you the enemy. Duplicity infects us all."

It had not escaped me that Chinese medicine includes the faeces of flying foxes, served as food.

"Look at it differently," I said. "Fungi, stones, trees and plants are indivisible. I am part of this nexus. More than you will ever be. Put it to a vote. Elect me or dispose of me."

To my surprise, they elected me.

"To change man's behaviour requires coercion," I said. "China is capable of such things."

The Pangolin replied with heartfelt sincerity, "The only way to stop mankind is to kill them. So it will be starvation, disease, magic, or war."

"If we starve them, they will eat us all," I said apologetically. "Can't we start with something simple like cleaning streams and oceans which are continuously degraded by man? Clean them and let fish and eels flourish.

"Or," I suggested, "let's research the noise we are making that interferes with the navigation of birds, eels and turtles unable to see the magnetic field.

"Or then again, let's campaign to reduce the human population.

"There are just too many. As America devours the planet, it is only right surplus population be channelled direct to America, always hungry for impoverished immigrants. Start with India. And put a cap on reproduction."

The Professor, not unreasonably, ignored me. He spoke of the Mao famine. "People ate grass, sawdust, leather, seeds plucked out of shit, tree trunks, even the dead. Mice, insects, everything. Terrifying stories circulated; men eating nests of birds alive; selling their children, but with the proceeds, eating other people's."

I began to weep. I hated him. My soul turned to God. Forgive us, oh God of Life. We fail to make amends. Forgive us for hunger.

Pericles echoed my feelings. "What happened in China was a curse upon men. They commemorate their suffering in terrible ways. They turned bush meat into a shibboleth wrested from the wizard Mao. In China, food became awakening.

"People sought folk medicine, ancient, embedded in the psyche. You want heart? Eat one. Better still, eat a worm. They have five hearts, or is it six? Drink blood. Eat liver; it will make you strong. Anything, everything, was eaten. Of course, modern Chinese people disown this, and rightly so."

The Pangolin spoke again in his modest way. "We need cast-iron guarantees China will stop importing wild animals. And civet breeding."

"Fat chance," someone said. It might have been me. "I have heard that State Enterprises in China have enormous debts. The leadership are suffering from paranoia. We must not see their unquestioned success as unquestionable. Thanks to the one-baby strategy, they are short of workers. GDP will drop like a stone."

"They are erratic," said the Pangolin.

I like Pangolins. Nocturnal, they live in trees as I do; they have been brutalised to fuel Chinese medicine, for improved lactation and blood flow.

Up spoke the little bat. "I can announce we have a crack force of viruses who can annihilate man. We have trained them to jump species. It's called the Zoonotic Squadron. Mink, Pigs, Sheep, Hens, Cows, Cats and Dogs are helping us, willing to host mutating viruses.

"We have been in touch with the bat section of the CCP. The communists are turning human, so the bats plan to break away and join us instead."

"What is the other option?"

"Hypnotise them," said Ursula, "'til their minds are full of darkness."

"But what actions are required?"

"The CCP have the techniques and power to help us," said the Professor.

The snake suggested nuclear war. "This is the only strategy. We know animals can survive the holocaust."

"What animals?"

"Cockroaches, scorpions, fruit flies, Barcoding wasps, Water bears, Mummichogs, *Deinococcus radiodurans*. All bomb proof."

"So, not real animals. Not like us."

"Cockroaches are intelligent!"

"But red-blooded animals?"

Things Fall Apart was affronted. "Perhaps you do not realise some animals have green blood, some blue, some yellow or brown. Lobsters, Octopuses, squids, horseshoe crabs, have copper-based blue blood. This nonsense about red blood is racism. Take care."

"Will animals with brains get wiped out?"

"You know insects have no brains?"

"They do. Did you not see *Men in Black*? Some have several brains. A brain for their antennae. One for the eyes. A brain for each leg. If a leg brain fails, they fall over. But when they inherit the earth, then will they be cleverer than humans?"

"Don't use that word 'evolve'," said Pericles. "First the dinosaurs, then humans, now insects. What does evolution have to do with any of it?"

"How do we get our story across to the Chinese?" asked the Pangolin.

"You had dealings with a Shaman in Russia; am I right?" he said. "The nuclear strategy pays back humanity in their own coin."

"How can we contain nuclear war?"

"Work with the USA, but isolate them. Get them to do our bidding, like the Israelis have done. The USA wish to be the superpower. They lost claim to that by racism, imperialism and duplicity. China will take them on eventually, but through proxies. A nuclear conflict will set humans back by a thousand years. Maybe less. The Wild will get respite. A steely China will preclude US adventurism. A localised Nuclear War, carefully designed, will take all other bets off the table. Those who trade in the technology can then be thrown into the river in a bag of scorpions, black mambas, pirañas and a cat."

The Professor interrupted. "I am from the New World. The Americans piss me off. They are richer than everyone. They have more nuclear weapons. And they have been victors in two world wars. But they are wrong about everything else. There is a simpler way. Make the Forests sacrosanct. Just work harder to keep the old ways alive."

"Then let's launch a Clan initiative. JOIN A CLAN, SAVE A SPECIES, inviting people everywhere to adopt a totem and save Nature."

"If it doesn't work, can we have war?"

"Yes."

"That's good enough for me," I said.

My team drew the idea to the UN's attention, who launched their own version. It went viral. New clans were formed everywhere. They adopted all sorts of totems, including Cannabis and Holstein cattle. People took taboo and totem seriously, including the pollution of waterways and deforestation.

The UN brand, once in tatters, perked up.

But I was out of sorts.

"Something terrible is about to happen," I told Annie.

"What? Another epidemic?"

"Far worse. A death cult."

"Heavy metal type of thing?"

"Charles Darwin type of thing."

"What on earth do you mean?"

"Darwin and his followers were progressives. By gradual improvement, slow morphing forms outperform those failing to adapt, who die. Humans think they are the magnificent outcome of this system. But if man forces the demise of other species, then Spencer's and Darwin's dark intentions are revealed."

"Oh, rubbish. It stands to reason," said Annie, "if a species goes extinct, it is not fit for purpose. There are innumerable reasons why we die. Rarely of extinction."

"Every species that goes extinct becomes a celebration of Darwinian cleansing, does it not?"

"What's so terrible about that?"

"One wrong step, one wrong definition, and man's monstrous narcissism is set free to unearth the planet, uproot the forests, debase biodiversity, making extinction not a *memento mori*, but the triumph of humans exonerating themselves for global warming, for ever chemicals, bottom trawling, big game hunting, greedy farming, destruction of forests, and mere murder, making man's tenure more lethal."

"My dear one," I pleaded, "we are committed to save Nature. I see magic in the natural world. I respect your disbelief, but magic is the renewal and inspiriting of Nature."

"I know. You think God is Life. I don't."

"You are a materialist," I said, gently. "I know you want to protect the world. But there are many others who destroy enchantment, out of spite and dogma..

I feel that you are changing, and in these terrible days you will come closer to religion. Let us work together in the end days?"

"The genome," she said, "is the only stepping stone for crossing over and reawakening. But there will never be just reason for any war."

"Oh, there is. Again and again you look to China, Annie. But remember, it is not the country or the people you admire, but the party. To solve a worldwide problem, a party must be built worldwide."

"The CCP was hardened off and made stern and perpetual by war. War is the engine of their revolution."

"No," I said. "We need togetherness, stability, and escape from profligacy."

A few days later, I met the Major. "'Join a clan' is failing," I said.

"I have migraines," he said.

"I'm sorry?"

"It is stress. Maybe lack of sex."

"Sorry?"

"My dad's were cured by love. In the Wild, there is musth. Young bulls controlled by alpha males. There is virtue in biology."

In my mind's eye, I saw the striped bees swarm on sweet musth.[15]

In the Zoo, things got worse. The clan initiative failed. An old stalwart said, "Why don't you leave the planet?"

I was sampling my medicines. There was a note from Eleniya's mother, who sent regards from the Khakha woman. I dosed myself heavily. Gratifyingly, the world changed. The Zoo took on a different aspect. The animals appeared invincible.

Trying to get to know my kids, I read up on jaguars and pumas in the Cordilleras of Chile and in Peru all the way up to the snow-line. There they eat guanacos. In the Amazon, they climb trees to hunt monkeys. In the pampas, sheep and horses are attacked. What struck me was how these predators are universally beautiful. Maybe my mind discerns beauty in death. Then, one day, the cubs were stolen. I went loco. Innocent children are a kind of rennet which set human sin. When Imperial Spain joined hands with Rome, they forbad child sacrifice. Closer to home, nuns exacted punishment for sinful pregnancies. Babies dropped in sewers. Sacrifice?

I thought of human mothers, their babies snatched from them, and I thought again of motherhood as the secret.

But my mind loops in chaotic spirals.

Satin in animal form returns enraged, searching for her cubs.

"You have failed me," she roared. "Return my cubs or I will put the curse of death upon you."

"Pericles has committed us to war."

"I care not. I have learned mysteries that turn all that grows green into black; that turns blood to black; that turns the air above to black. Man casts a blight on the earth. Find me my young."

I saw her then as immense, supernatural, defeating all enemies no matter who.

The Professor declared War in front of the cage in which a courtship dance had begun. The birds of paradise looked amazed.

"I want a record of this momentous day," he proclaimed. "I want your Paradisiac designs exhibited in the British Museum, including your feathers and some pretty taxidermy."

Despite the threat, the courting birds gave short shrift. He spoke loudly. "I command you. Design the emblems, colours, standards and guidons of my regiments."

But the birds got on with love. Birds are the most beautiful of living things and make me wish I could have seen their ancestors, who came from nowhere and returned there millions of years past.

Pericles is on parade, a model of a Major-General. His preparations are moving fast. A foolhardy young horse, caught eating sugar from a human hand, is fed to carnivores. First to die, he will be celebrated, not for stabbing humanity in the back, or killing innocent bystanders in God's name, but as a martyr.

A new day. A cool wind blows...

Inexplicably, it is mild, the sunshine sweet and the air clean. In Egerton, the Plain Tree is white. In the far distance, misty and faint, the great sky touches the hills, and lends them something blue.

Huge clouds gather above. They march to the winds' stirring music. A growling echoes just above the house, as if within the heavenly overgrowth a Tiger hides. A few spots of rain fall. I feel them cold on my cheek. In the walled garden, I write a letter to my father, whose love I crave. I make a prayer for those about to walk the path of mortality. Wood pigeons repetitively mouth their propaganda, a recital of unnerving repetition: who, who, who knows the unknown?

In the distance, I hear a sad and melancholic dirge of dogs wailing at their exclusion from the hunt.

Increasingly nervous, I take to my secret store of substances; and so begin powerful visions. It is about now I receive a further batch of treats based on good old Fly Agaric, and my perceptions take a different turn. A red light suffuses my mind.

Ulysses asks after my cubs. "Did they not sleep beneath your bed?"

"I tried to keep them safe."

But now Ulysses is the enemy. I see his mind stretched thinly over the sinkhole of indifference.

"The war is coming," I tell Annie.

"Who could possibly support that?"

"Best you go away."

"If it's war, where are the Americans?"

"Not this time."

"Who, then?"

"China."

"But you hate them."

"Do I?"

"Are you involved?"

"Yes," I said.

"I'll tell my psychiatrist. Don't be surprised if you end up sectioned."

I called in on Clementine.

"Come in, come in," she said warmly. "Would you like some weed?"

"A reporter called O'Divoleen," I explained.

"I know him."

"He writes of a man who prowls the Zoo at night, with access to the animals, sedating them, plying them with substances, crying and grunting, attempting intercourse."

"I don't like the sound of that. To be frank, Annie's father and I think the job has affected her mental health."

The Animals take up position against Adam.

Where are the enemy? Hiding indoors. The streets are quiet. The new blocks beside the river are empty. Rumour has it action started a week ago, when the rich in Belgravia faced an incursion of rats. First blood to us.

I take stock.

I pray for Annie. She is a good woman, denied the experience of motherhood. Why? Politics are her Achilles' heel. Could she really be in love with me? Could I be in love with her? It was a bitter thought. I was a blight upon her life. I feel for a moment an intense flood of love.

I reflect on Pericles. I feel no love for him. He is lonely and will be punished.

The light dims.

I pray for Satin. She inhabits two worlds, transcending both. Metaphysical, and life eternal.

Everywhere contradictions.

I check to see if a last-minute change of heart has happened. Annie's father contacts me.

"Annie speaks of peril. As an Englishman, I invoke God and America, both of whom have served me."

"Surely not."

"I don't want to intrude, but Annie is my daughter. I must ask you to stay away until your situation is resolved."

"No problem," I reply. "I will involve her no further. Give her my love."

"The Chinese made solemn undertakings on Hong Kong. Don't trust them. The Chinese Communist Party are hostage to ideology. They can't be trusted."

"I am an observer, no more…"

Just then, an old man, thin and steely, rushes in. Bloodless, cold eyes half-closed, he speaks.

"You are," he says, "in time to hear my research."

"This is the Headquarters of the joint staff of the combined Armies of the Animal Kingdom," I reply.

I had been practising this all day.

He clears his throat. "My name is Sentinel," he said. "I work for the University for Peace."

"Ah? United Nations? Good luck."

"My research is on Alpha males."

"No alpha females?"

"The whole community."

"How do you measure this?"

"Are you familiar with fission fusion?"

"Yes. Centripetal. Centrifugal. Contrapuntal. One Alpha male atop the whole. Alpha males and females atop each sub-section?"

The alpha male is privileged.

"Alpha males are supported by older females," he said crisply.

"A pact?"

"Dominance over the whole community, unified by the alpha network. The rest submit."

"We have well-trained troops. Do we need Alphas?"

"You need to be ruled. Stalin hosted Mao and had his faeces secretly examined for androgens, glucocorticoids. Mao's testosterone was elevated."

"Out of interest, Stalin took the same test, in private. Same result."

"Any downside?"

"Stalin had elevated testosterone and glucocorticoids simultaneously. He disrupted his government to create instability. This prolonged his dominance.

"Knowingly or not, the party organised for this. A parallel narrative emerges around Mao and is thought to explain his extreme policies."

"The costs of dominance played out badly in both men, notably in the immunosuppressive records and in high levels of aggression and risk-taking. Too high."

"But prolonged leadership in both cases. Extremely bloody."

"How did they get away with it?"

"Those who survived paid in obeisance. Others died in fear."

"It seems…"

"Yes?"

"As if human organisations may be determined genetically and hormonally. Alphas seek dominance in fighting, foraging…"

"We looked into human beliefs," he said. "Indian colleagues suggest something similar. They include the centralising role."

"This sounds like religion. Does it have a bearing – forgive my rudeness – on the war in which our lives are forfeit?" I asked.

"Animals – and humans – point to hormonal agency."

"I know what you are going to say," I surmised. "Edit the genome? Create stability? No time for that."

"Coercion is the last throw."

"I prefer death to ideas unproven."

"What if God failed to message us?"

"What if we are deaf?" he said.

Chapter Sixteen

We opened like a flower unfolding in silence, then to the loud trumpets of Brugmansia.

"What is that?" squeaks a nervous rat.

The immense figure of a Polar Bear looms into view, limping and radiating terror. She marches along, daring humanity to confront her.

What if she is pregnant? Can Science enter her, an antigen which will challenge her very being?

I mourn for her. In Nature, she would have coupled with some Behemoth, the embodiment of violence, and then, before birthing, would flee him and his sex to protect her children from infanticide. And so in the vast wastes, in terrible hunger, she would barely live, scarcely surviving save for the immensity of her maternity. She is, against all prejudice, a goddess.

But now, forced to endure captivity, her intense needs made worse by the machinations of Ulysses and his experiments, she has found her way to the front line. She draws the enemy's fire, longing for death.

Behind her, the Schwerpunkt is mustering. Its target: the soft centre of human avarice, the City of London.

Microbes, under the flag of Pathogen, are deployed in invisibility. They strike when the enemy drops his guard.

The war is underway in the air, where hysteria shrieks overhead.

The left wing is far out in the Atlantic. As officers, the killer whales drive sharks before them, in shore. Unbeknownst to humans, the killer whales, long held back, are free to hunt humanity even on the beaches and the landing grounds.

Snakes slide out of the forests, led by the giant anaconda.

On the right wing in the Americas are coyotes, jackals, wolves, wild dogs; and in Africa, hyenas. Big cats are drafted in as honorary canidae. Bears come close behind. Each has a silver bullet which will protect them against the pitiful rifles of humanity.

In the centre, the hornets, wasps, bees, and spiders use camouflage to occupy man's sheets; and in the bathrooms, towels.

Tarantulas, killer ants, and scorpions await the enemy in lavatories.

These moves cause panic. Once microbes are released, the immune systems of humanity will have no time to adjust to new diseases. Panic will turn into depression when it is clear nature is afoot.

The schwerpunkt is concentrated, too quick, too deadly for humans to repel: a billion tiny, perfectly formed infantrymen, the micropunkts on parade have been superbly drilled in the belly of India.

Before the storm broke, our propaganda forewarned bloodshed overwhelming all.

Surprisingly, a great alliance with the Chinese Communist Party is announced by Pericles. The CCP and the Wild fight side by side against democracy, which hubristically is aligned against them.

And now reports come in of new combatants. Thousands of animals shipped out of China, huge in size, include a kind of rhinoceros with enlarged head, enormous ears, and a long, long unicorn. They are the Chinese token of good faith and gene editing. In parallel, dense clouds of cockatoos fly in, with beaks like horns.

The Chinese had read the runes long ago. These creatures are the product of much science.

This morphogenesis baffles the enemy. As in a trance, a few imaginatively glimpse the spirit world, its mysteries, its curses. The rest drown in magic.

Against expectation, new allies of the Wild enter the battle. Boreas, and his icy blast from the Arctic and the Shaboob and Shamal howl in burning rage out of the deserts.

In the Amazonian state of Paránormal, President Impresario pronounces, "The Indigenous in their reservations are animals in a net." Or did he say Zoo? Is he marking the last event of history as land-rights activists are mercilessly killed by police?

Newspapers announce: 'Landowners continue to contract off-duty police officers to perform extrajudicial killings and land evictions.' A few poor families from the

Liga dos Camponeses Pobres cling to rights officially delisted. They will fail.

The confiscation of their lands will proceed until the gallimaufry of the Wild is exterminated.

Hubris nourishes the old instinct to dissimulate even in the face of death. It has voided vestigial consciences and, at the last trump, will evacuate even those last tiny remnants of virtue hidden in their bowels, before being drawn back into self-centredness.

Their house of glass shattering, cuts itself in two, man and spirit severed.

A proclamation is published. The guilt is Humanity's. They face unceasing War. They must retreat from the forest, or will be slain in pouring darkness. Their schisms, their exceptionalisms will not save them.

They surrender, doomed in their materialism and mendacity. Or fevered, and in despair, they hide.

"This," cries Kali, "heralds the world's end." Her voice reaches the moon, the stars.

In the street already lie the dead, foremost the huge Pericles. How did he get there? What makes him shine so brightly, as luminous as the moon-lit ocean from which he came?

His vast bulk is a hill over which troops march, unseeing and terrified, to enact his orders.

Poor Pericles, how unseemly is your end. Despite your death, I can hear your voice from yesterday.

"Humanity in its second and last coming is vanquished," he had cried. "Let churchmen set this to music.

"They have mistaken their ascendancy. They destroyed our Earth. Dressed in the bright armour of progressive anthropocentrism, humanity adorns itself in fragmented morality and half-truths. Books about themselves crowd the minds of these refugees from truth. Their leaders meet, in pomp, in regalia, woven out of plunder and poverty. They turn their backs on justice and pump their children up on the catwalk of their greed. They will be silenced."

Thus Pericles spoke before he fell. I mourn him. I love him now. Yet he is a falling echo. For I hear on the wind a new chorus of voices, a paean to the Goddess of pandemonium.

After that, a blur. I hear screams. Ulysses stumbles blindly into me. I run through the Zoo. The dead lie everywhere. Things fall apart, Loopkins, Anita. My heart stops.

A rat shitting on the tarmac looks at the clouds unfolding.

"What news?" I call. "Is the battle won?"

"What battle?"

"To the death?"

"Oh, that," it said.

When I got to my bed, I took another look to check my stash.

I slept fitfully. And I dreamt a dream that cleansed me. All the hallucinogens I consumed these last weeks drained away. And yet…

I saw a fungus that grew beside the roads and motorways. And from the supersized gantries hung men, clearly still alive, twisting and bucking in the middle air. And out of the men grew fruiting bodies that swayed and spewed out clouds of spore. I awoke and realised I was screaming. It was the living, waking morrow. For conscience had emerged out of the forest; and brought its message. The message was my dream. The Fungus has a weapon honed to suit its enemy, who it now shapes perfectly as a zombie.

Satin's cage is empty. So silent. So empty save for dust, which swirls in the wind. Yet I know she is close by, in rage uncontrollable.

Here she comes, seemingly calm.

"Where are my children?" she asks. "Are they paraded by my enemies?"

"The media will tell us soon enough," I whispered, "for they are long since suborned by the climacteric. Wait for me, my love. I will be a moment."

I raid the offices at the Zoo and there amongst the paperwork I find what I did not want to find. '*Panthera onca*, two cubs, four weeks. To be culled, because hybrid.'

What? What could this mean? 'Culled because hybrid'? I scrabble in papers and files.

A further handwritten note says: 'The hunter-gatherers turned pastoralists. Farms scaled to kingdoms;

begat armies, obeyed hierarchies. The minds of men now swarm with dogs, nets, snakes, fire, swords, conquest.'

God, I thought, not the great power beyond knowledge, but humanity's dry lobbying apotheosis of itself, commands it.

Death increases his kingdom.

Then I see a chart. Beneath, the following words in black ink:

'Two Arabian Oryx put down. Oryx died at Edinburgh and London zoos in 2000 and 2001. Private zoo, Jaguar hybrid cubs. 2025, put down. Unviable.

'We failed to install foolproof security,' it read.

I shout. I rage.

Read the shibboleths of men I cry. They despise. The spirits will be avenged.

I turn to Satin. Humans and animal long since parted. The rift will not be healed. I pray those with life eternal guard our children.

That is just worthless human words.

All my forebodings rush in.

"Who dared?" she said, lips arching over great fangs.

"The Zoo," I said. "The Zoo."

"No," she roars. "In the world below, one hundred and ninety human tribes meet in pitch darkness. I alone will descend into that pit. If they have a God, I will devour him."

Though I have long known her in human form, she changed, her eyes large and staring, terrifying, unforgiving, remorseless, full of hate. It is this I have unleashed. My eyes are filled with tears.

"Forgive me," I say. "Our union does not compute."

She has gone, awakening he nightmare of the Amur Tiger.

I meet Ursula and blurt out our secret.

"She is the monster and a loving mother both," she replies. "Man's highest good is bought with crimes and paid in tears."

"I am not human," I admit. But that confession, too, is yet another promise broken.

In dance, in art, in music, in religion, the fibres of prehuman order can be discerned: of bower birds, and cockatoos, spiders, wolves, snake, ibis, crocodile, chimp and elephant.

Though we triumph, they are vanishing.

Time passed.

A kind of peace descended. As if memory repressed had, like a sweet spring, re-emerged to feed the past. Day followed upon day, in a seamless necklace of sunshine and showers. I found delight in a zephyr of calm liturgy and observances.

The Zoo was boarded up, the keepers gone. There was some creature in the place lingering on, neither animal nor human, a ghostly presence, uneasy, remorseful. Sometimes in the night it groaned.

As my hopes for Nature also groaned. Like some old man with a box of items, perversely rummaging through them, I held up one memory and now another, to review the world when it was fresh and sweet and it gave birth to love.

Lost loves. Eleniya, Satin, my shrew, only recall sadness. I mourned friends: Yamhead, the Major, Anita, Gia Mina, Timmy, Pericles.

But search though I may, there is no hope. Until, that is, they brought me Gaga's baby. For many months she had been making this beautiful child.

I sat in the sunlight and watched her playing with the baby.

To see her immersed in delight is for me a zenith. Whereas I have nothing; neither offspring, nor partner, nor any stuff saved for a rainy day. I have this vision.

Is it not wrong? A beautiful, serious woman denied motherhood?

Once human suitors, vile and absolute, slew and ate their enemy to show women they could furnish life in surplus.

A young mother giving birth early was thought to need replenishment by men. Her infant fed to her engenders this idea of savagery which evolved to sin.

***

My mind turned home.

Walking the woods, I saw far off a quarry, shining from behind black winter trees.

Are Germans not ingenious? They made trees and earth their workshop, where ships, and iron, and charcoal manufactured god.

I wandered on.

Then I came closer and saw a white scar, but no chalk there. By slow morphogenesis, a great swathe of blackthorn was displaying her tapestry of blossom, so pervasive I had imagined them to be a wall of chalk. Instead of chalk, there was an aggregate of tiny flowers, in such abundance they appeared as clouds of charm, white flower upon white flower, icons of spring.

My thoughts turned to my God who placed in me the natural recoil of spiritual rebirth. Peace and love took hold. How is it so many cannot grasp or respect the ubiquity and passion of our worship?

All they have to do is interrogate good people. I honour those who withstand the cynicism of corrosive minds.

Sir Alistair Hardy, the evolutionist, pursued his study of the spirit world with forensic zest. Why is he not remembered more respectfully?

He believed in Christianity and Science both. Many find the diatribes of vainglorious men more entertaining, less embarrassing.

In desperation, they invent a Meme; a metaphysical disease which befalls the weak. There is nothing scientific in such inventions. Atheists study history, belief, art, worship. Do they not? The believer respects any atheist willing to renounce credulity, materialism: sin, not least greed, which fuels attacks upon Nature, and such cyclic errors.

Everywhere is greed. You hear it in low talk of wealth. It makes roads smooth, opens landscapes: builds homes, neither good nor bad, save if they savage Nature.

I saw the blackthorn glimmering, its bright clouds calling to animals to come closer, each tiny flower a charm, a quark, in Nature's collaboration. White flower upon white flower upon white flower. It is the soft mysterious call of heaven where larks sing: do not forget.

God ordains the terrors, but also the exquisite synergy of the living world. Of course there is evil. But a host of spirits inspired by God confront it.

After such joys, I sought redemption but found none. Do animals, like men, yield to absolution? Without forgiveness, I am lost. I will ask the Pontiff for an audience.

'Blake, in his day,' I wrote, 'stood for the imagination. Palmer painted a golden glimmering light of paradise amidst brooding shadows. Somehow he failed. Is Nature so desacralised, we cannot unite with one another? Will you agree to meet and see if we can work together?'

He sent back a note agreeing to a meeting, but gently suggesting my ideas were not original.

I was sitting in his waiting room when I heard a low guttural sound, something I once heard in hospital, a noise of suffering, of pneumonia.

I then heard a high-pitched sound like tyres in an emergency. I stood up and walked into reception. His secretary was working at her desk.

Maybe she heard nothing.

There was another sound.

She removed an earpiece.

"Sorry?" she said.

"A sound."

"A sound?"

"Yes. Would you like to check?"

"It's OK. You are free to go in."

The office was in use. No-one was there. The condition of the room spoke humility. Much expenditure elsewhere caused old assets such as these to be abandoned. Dark panelling in need of improvement. A painting dated MDCXCI upon the wall. A Tudor toilet cupboard untidy in disuse. Then I noticed the white face.

Beneath the desk. A white face.

No sign of damage.

A storm struck, then blew clean away.

A spirit had escaped.

One hand, blue-veined, clutched a Bible.

On the neck, lacerations, bleeding from the jugular, horribly in view.

Above the mantelpiece, a print. In the distance, a golden sea. To the left, Elysian fields. Visions that enthralled poets of another era. Blake, they say, evidenced the elastic nervous spring of uncaged spirits. Who has been uncaged?

When I got home, I reread the letter. 'Do not lament the loss of the pastoral, nor the decline of Virgil,' it said. 'With initiatives such as yours, all will be well. There is so much in the Bible that chimes with your idea. I am sure the church can share a platform.

'You might care to read the pamphlet I enclose. A joint event sponsored by the Royal Society. By the way, I am not familiar with the term "Hebu". Perhaps you will elucidate when we meet.'

***

Humanity, it appears, has more to do. Genes get man to base camp, at the age of twelve. Most then remain still in childhood ten years or more, before they grasp the rudiments of society and of nature.

Humans, like gods, drive extinction. They waste their early years on fashion, music, materialism. But neither the natural world, nor truth.

Without a different apprenticeship, they will destroy themselves.

The fourth law, as proposed, says behavioural traits are associated with many variants. Each accounts for but a dash of variability. It can take many genetic variants to produce just one trait.

In the current crisis, all life is so imperfect, especially mankind's. The only chance of change is by consent.

There is the wider complexity accounted for by family. I have the image of a youngster in my mind, applying for a job as a paid-up accredited human being.

Genes are just his starting point. Evolution has prepared him to treat Nature with contempt.

Will he spend his life gazing into the mirror of his species? Is vanity the primum mobile of his life?

Make a bonfire of his liberties.

Unexpectedly, Annie arrived.

"I heard you were leaving, so wrote something to catch the moment."

"Good. Good. A poem?"

"An Epilogue," she said.

"Oh," I replied.

In a clear strong voice, she recited: "In *Animal Farm*, they started in lock step with humans. Men departed. Animals remained as slaves.

"Mankind's cartels keep the majority quiet, feeding them Human Rights, and flesh from animals that never lived.

"Materialism seized undeserved rewards."

I nodded. "Our only Hope is Equality between Nature and Humanity."

"Heebie, listen. Give up this delusion. You are not an animal. My Doctor says so."

"What shall I do?"

"Be Nature's sweetheart. You are set against mankind, Heebie, which is wrong of you."

"Man will not rescue Nature. They have unfathomable bad faith."

"There are more good people than you conceive of."

"Democracy…," I began.

"We know about democracy. Step back and start again. Which system will change the world?"

"We do not want dictators."

"In China, a new middle class has arisen, and with it brand new morality."

"Mao wanted Kruschev to start a nuclear war," I countered. "Do you need more proof?"

"In Chinese DNA is Taoism," she replied. "Taoism is at heart Nature. The Chinese now are open to change. Infect them with compassion."

"Can you not feel my fear? Must we go back to slavery?" I pleaded. "In China, Orwell is banned."

"They are not slavers, but obedient."

"Was not your Eleniya offered to the Amur tiger as a hostage? Let men swear oaths to give up lives for Nature."

"We need less people. Less people will consume less Nature. The USA, dependent on immigration to keep their defective system going, will be cornered in the end by socialism. Educate them for the greater good."

"And if they do not heed?"

"Tell them the ants are coming. The most damaging invasive species in the world will wreak havoc. As a foretaste of ant civilisations, the fire ant can host up to two hundred queens in a single colony. The Yellow Mad ant invaded Christmas Island, reaching seventy million in fifteen years, and killed fifteen million land crabs with formic acid."

"The last resort will be to poison them and so poison Nature," I said.

"I am glad you take me seriously, Heebie. Marry me. Let me make a son. I have longed for this."

"Annie, you cannot tidy Eden. You cannot miniaturise Forests, or belittle forest life. I worship a God for whom all life is sacred."

"Oh, I know you," she replied tearfully. "You want to have Eleusinian mysteries. You want to go back before Christ. If you marry me, we can make a child, invincible, a peacemaker."

"You are too much for me, dear Annie."

I went my way.

Three years pass.

The same restaurant now empty.

I am getting old. I manfully shake a napkin over my lap.

"Have you come to terms?"

"Terms?"

"Did you seek treatment?"

"What for?"

"Your psychosis."

"Psychosis? The mind ensnared, like an animal in a zoo? Hardly. I hold you in high regard, Annie, more than any one. In truth, I love you and always have. But long ago

I came to terms. What matters to me are forests. The rest means nothing. Though the planet dies, my soul will not."

"You love delusions, fuelled by substances, do you not?" she replied. "What have we now? A globe barely surviving. A war lost; animals defeated. Everyone, save you, agrees the cause. The fifth great lie."

"What lie?"

"Like asteroids, these lies periodically shatter earth. Louis XIV taught Hitler. Marx. Trump. Each lie changes mankind a little for the worse, moving onward inexorably towards great and irreducible extinction."

"What is this lie?"

"That a conspiracy by science discredits our inherited belief in Nature."

"The animals surrendered when the Chinese stood back. It seems Marxism is equality."

"Poor dear animals. It is clear to me that scientists are trained to disbelieve. Belief means reaching out beyond mere proof to defend each forest; to protect each life against extinction. The lie promotes and aggrandises those previously forgotten. But never Nature."

"China is one of us now," she protested. "They are hungry for choice," she insisted.

"Do they show compassion?"

"We all want compassion."

"And the Uighars?"

"Opponents. Not for us to judge."

Same old Annie.

"Are needs now scientifically arranged?"

"The new plan is to break the planet up," she said. "Forests will not recover. Monocultures will fail. Ebony, Oak, Rosewood, Ash will vanish in a million bonfires."

"Surely not."

She weeps.

Then, to my dismay, Venetsianov appears. He kisses her lightly on the cheek and shakes my hand.

I laugh, and put my menu down. "I am in a mangrove swamp," I say. "I will not eat, but breathe the sea mist. On the Ocean's edge I'll sing."

"You will do well," says Venetsianov. "In waters of aquamarine, tiny creatures forge oxygen for Mother Earth.

"And down below, in the vast deep, the behemoths multiply and sequester carbon in unimaginable quantities."

"Can you see that bird upon the mangrove tree?" I ask. "'The Taliban have a nuclear device,' the bird is saying. 'Iran has a nuclear device.'"

"So, too, does Saudi," says Venetsianov.

"Mankind has had its chance," is my reply. "Coercion failed. Let Nature protect herself. A book is opening on the future. For thirty million years, songbirds were island hopping, changing beaks, diversifying. How many beaks have there been? The idea it takes that time is laughable. Life courts danger, invents new forms. Life recapitulates. The choreography is immense, involving every dancer."

I appeal to Annie.

"We are indissoluble, you and I."

"But you've retired." She laughs.

He takes her hand in triumph. My heart sinks.

"We understand," he says. "You think our lives are but shadows of an ideal world. I am a proud Russian. We alone can save the planet. Life, as you know, is finite. Death comes closer. Biodiversity for a while forestalled it. Your democracy, a sideshow, killed Socrates with lies. Things change. Things become. We dwell in the real world. We will be its masters."

Annie squeezes his hand. Smiling, she says, "I love you, Heeb."

Then she adds, "I'm with the Prince."